T0354515

BREAST GHOST

For book orders, email orders@traffordpublishing.com.sg

Most Trafford Singapore titles are also available at major online book retailers.

Printed in Singapore.

ISBN: 978-1-4669-9899-5 (sc)
ISBN: 978-1-4669-9898-8 (e)

Trafford rev. 09/05/2013

 www.traffordpublishing.com.sg
Singapore
toll-free: 800 101 2656 (Singapore)
Fax: 800 101 2656 (Singapore)

CONTENTS

PROLOGUE

"As fast as lightning, it swooped her up from the ground with her breasts and took off. It didn't Make use of it's hands at all. She felt she was flying round and round above her own house. She was trapped in between the cleavage, screaming and crying, unable to make any movement at all. While in the cleavage, she could feel the cool scaly and hairy skin of the ghost chest. And the smell almost make her throw up."

INTRODUCTION

Ghost in Asian countries are no different from the ghost from anywhere else in any other part of this world. However, in this region, many of these ghost stories are still being told from mouth to mouth. Unlike the Chinese, Hindoos, and Westerners who had had their ghosts stories recorded early in the century. Believers here sometimes refer to a ghost as theirs God, which are worshiped daily.

The Malays believe in ghosts. Though they asked protection from the Only ALLAH (God), some brave individuals always go hunting for ghosts. Many ghosts become their friend and slave. However, in the end themselves and their family and generations are placed in big trouble. It's still happening right until today.

The Chinese worshiped ghosts. If they found a tree or place where a strange thing occurred or where there had been some sighting, they would worship that tree or place. They would start to burn joss sticks and papers and make some offering. They would pray especially for protection, good luck and health. They even have a 'Ghost Month Festival' to celebrate. The Indians, scared of the ghost, prayed to their own Lord for protection and many other things in their daily lives.

The Caucasians, Westerners on the other hand, have the occasion to celebrate called Halloween, where they pretend to be a ghost, they dress up like a ghost, they make up their faces just like a ghost. In other words, they are not frightened of the ghost. The sighting of any strange being would always be classified as an Alien or a UFO encounter.

The stories that I'm going to tell you here may be a true encounter, a real-life experience or just a fiction. No one can confirm the authenticity of the stories. No one can tell whether it is true or not. Only the person who experienced it knows how scary it is to encounter those things behind the darkness of the night. All the stories are based in Singpaore, though there are one or two taken from our neighboring countries, Indonesia and Malaysia.

Let's take all the stories in this book as an entertainment only. Do not take the stories seriously. After all, these stories are happening in the Asian's community, especially the Malay. So sit back and relax. Do not be afraid. Don't take any of this as real.

BREAST GHOST 'WEWE GOMBEL'

Have you ever heard about 'Wewe Gombel' (Breast Ghost)? The name is very funny: 'Wewe' means Ghost and 'Gombel' means Breast; they are Javanese words. They are very real, and can be very mischievous. If you are as old as me (half a decade) now, you surely would have heard about it. You probably had been introduced to this ghost as young as six years old. Your parents, relatives or neighbors would have told you about 'Wewe Gombel' the naked lady ghost with a big bosom who like to snatch little children.

She liked to hide children who strayed alone, especially during the sunset. How far this was true, nobody would be able to confirm. I have never seen it personally. I also never heard people around me

1

having any kind of experience with this ghost except with regard to the story which I'm writing to entertain your mind, in detail below.

It was a common understanding that 'Wewe Gombel' meant no harm to the children. It was just a warning to the parents to look after their children properly. However, she might hide the children for a few hours, days or weeks, which might cause some health problems. Hunger was not the question as she would feed them generously, but only with shit and maggots. Their beverage would be urine. Believe me, the children would be forced to eat and drink it. Of course the feast looked much more delicious.

When people started to seriously look for the lost little child, then she would release him/her. That poor child would be in trauma and get a serious health problem which might have led to death if he/she had been kept by the ghost for a longer period of time. There was no case where this ghost had ever been caught. They were very elusive and would hide after releasing the child.

It's not easy for a mother to keep an eye on six, seven and more children. Some of them can be very mischievous and too adventurous. The parent, especially the mother is responsible in case anything happened to them. This ghost story is meant to frighten the kids from playing truant, especially during the twilight time. In order to keep them away from trouble, the mother would tell them not to go far away, or they may be caught by this 'Wewe Gombel', and would be fed with faeces and maggots

Ghost stories to some extent are very effective only to little children. Once they reach the teenage year they wouldn't care so much about ghosts, or maybe they've forgotten about them, except for the few who are really timid. So they would start to roam around further away from their house and village.

Every ghost story had its origin. Unlike many other parts of the world that had became literate long ago, where many of their stories were recorded in books, including ghost stories from more than thousands of years ago. The story and legend in many countries in the South East Asian Region are told from a mouth to mouth. Therefore, oftens the story became distorted or changed into many versions, and we can never guess which one is the original. Below is one version of one tale.

Long long ago in one of the villages in Central Java, Indonesia, there lived a newly married couple. They we're a very happy and loving couple. However, many years after they got married, they had yet to be granted with any children.

After ten years, the husband's patience wore off. He started to feel sad and bored. The wife could sense that the husband was not at ease. Even so, what to do? They had seen a lot of 'Bomoh' (spiritual healers) and had made all kinds of offerings. They also had spent a lot of time and money, but their wishes were still not granted. Secretly, the husband kept another woman in the same village.

Though the wife was suspicious, she didn't have any clue or evidence to accuse him. When confronted, the husband completely denied the wrongdoing. However, the villagers came to know about the man's unfaithfulness which was against their culture at that time.

One day they caught him red handed, and beat him up. The wife begged for mercy on behalf of the husband. But nobody listened to her. They continued to batter him to death in front of her eyes. She couldn't do anything except howl and cry until she had no more tears to shed. Her tears dried after the villagers buried him; she became stressful and a little crazy.

She would walk around the village looking for a house of people who had just given birth or those who had little children. When the children were alone, and nobody was around, she would snatch the little child and brought him/her home.

She would feed and care for them as if her own. She was caught few times snatching children from the street. The villagers warned her sternly. After the many stern warnings, she was not seen roaming the street village for some days. The villagers kept their children at home all the time. Actually, she did her works more discretely, in the twilight time only. Everyday she waited in ambush to catch those stray little kids.

One day she managed to catch a little toddler boy and brought him home. Somebody saw it and told the boy's parent. With some other villagers they immediately went to her house. True enough, she was cuddling the little boy and trying to feed the four-years-old kid when the boy's parents, and some villagers arrived on her door step. She was ostracised. She was asked to leave the village immediately or meet the same fate as her husband.

She left empty handed that same night wandering in the dark at the edge of the village, on the outskirst of the jungle. A few weeks later some villagers noticed that she would stand under a jackfruit tree near the village cemetery. Some saw her sitting on one of the branches with her ragged dress. Many kind people left some food and clothes for her.

She never touched it at all. She wouldn't trust anybody. She survive by eating fruits she found in the jungle. What they did not know was that she was still longing and hoping to catch a kid. She became more and more dirty. Her ragged clothing barely covered her body, showing up her big bosom. Her hair was also unkempt;

she looked like a ghost, and thus she was nicknamed 'Wewe Gombel'—The Breast Ghost.

By then the whole village were watching, and strictly instructed their children to stay at home, especially near sunset time. Some time later, they would still occasionally see her at the same place. They didn't expect her to survive there alone.

However no one could confirm whether the almost naked big bosom lady was human or ghost now. She never talked to anyone, and no one there went close to her. She just stood like a statue at various locations in the cemetery area. Fortunately, no children had been reported missing for quiet a long time in the area

In the early seventies, there was news that shook not only the Java Barat area, but also the whole of Java. 'Wewe Gombel' kidnapped a six-years-old girl. The news spread from a mouth to mouth, it spread very fast like a virus, and traveled to far away regions, faster than the news from the newspaper 'Wewe Gombel' has struck again. Beware!! This is a real story, let's read on?

It happened in a remote village called Jati Luhur in West Java. Many people knew about this story. At that time, the surrounding of this village was still thick jungle. The houses there were far apart, and at night, it was really pitch dark. This is the experienced of a six-years-old girl told by an Indonesian maid.

One evening, nearing sunset time, this six-years-old girl was going to the bathroom which was about twenty meters behind her house, Suddenly, she saw a big dark figure in a squatting position with her back facing her near the bathroom door. The figure was struggling with something. She stopped and stared at the figure, trying to think what it was.

She said at that moment the figure suddenly turned around and stood up. Under the minimum light of the last sun's ray, she could see a very tall black lady with long unkempt hair looking down at her. She could see that her breasts were hung down to her knees. She also saw that the figure was struggling with a small animal in her cleavages. It was the family cat. She lets the cat go immediately she saw her.

She was stunned and screamed for help as loud as she could. She could see more clearly, and for sure the face was real dark and ugly. Its mouth was so big with fangs. Its red eyes were bulging out and almost popped out of their sockets. Most certain this creature was naked.

As quick as lightning, it swooped her up from the ground with her breasts and took off. It didn't make use of its hands at all. She felt she was flying around and round above her own house. She was trapped in between the cleavage screaming and crying, unable to make any movement at all. In the uncomfortable cleavage, she could feel the cool scaly and hairy skin of the ghost's chest. And the smell almost make her throw up.

From the top, she could see some people, possibly her parents and sibling busily shouting and searching for her. She screamed back and crying, but nobody could hear her. Although at the time it was hovering lower, about just a meter above their head, they couldn't see or hear her shouting. She could hear the commotion near her house. Some villagers started to gather at her house as the village emergency drums sounded.

As it flew higher she could see her own house get smaller; then she could see the shapes of the houses in the whole village. She became too frightened and fainted. Laughing, the ghost drifted, flying further away from her house. Some people who knew about the supernatural happenings, managed to trace the cunning ghost and they followed her on the ground. Within two hours they found it's hide-out. It released her, and a few minutes later she was found under a jackfruit tree.

They carried her home. When she regained consciousness, she described her experiences in great details. As she was so tired, she felt asleep. The next day she was still in some kind of trauma, and was also frightened to step out of the house. She stayed in all the time. She suffered a mental problem for a few years. However, with continuous spiritual treatment from some faith healers and strong moral support from her parents, family and the villagers, she finally recovered fully. Later in life she led a normal life, she got married and have few children.

Here is yet another version of the story of the 'Wewe Gombel', popularly known as 'Hantu Tetek' in this part of the region. The Breast Ghost prowled at dusk. Here, the ghost is known to attack adults too. Many unexplained deaths are sometime said to be related to being the victim of this ghost.

'Hantu Tetek' (Breast Ghost) is not choosy; boys and girls are it's equal prey, if they had strayed alone within its territory. She usually attacked those children who were still playing hide-and-seek after the twilight prayer call.

She uses her breasts to attack her victim and makes full use of her huge breasts to suffocate them to death or by placing their heads between her breasts to crush the delinquent skulls. Maybe, there was no tissue in them at all; they were pure muscle, reptilian, flecked with fungal patches of scales. When the ghost's nipples started to seek each other out, and united it would reach the maximum power. Between the breasts she could easily constrict even an adult head with an unbelievable power. However, there are many well known cases where she only hid them, and meant no harm at all.

Anyway, what a way to perish! Nose squashed against the sternum, ears wall presured by hot and scaly skin. A lot of blood oozed out of the mouth, nose, eyes and both ears when the body was found. On the other hand, perhaps a more profound death might be mysteriously hidden in the cleavage of the 'Hantu Tetek' instead of on the lap of the dear wife.

Sometimes, mistresses were being referred as 'Hantu Tetek'. As you know, they always hide someone's husband. They would release him when his wife was seriously looking for him. Besides the mistresses any woman with extraordinary big bosoms is also referred to as 'Hantu Tetek'—Breast Ghost.

Actresses and models are the most common ones. Don't be mistaken. This type of ghost is even more dangerous. They're mostly feared by married women. They are easily identified and very timid. Once their whereabouts is found they would release the men and go into hiding. If they were caught they would beg for mercy and promise to leave the men alone. Normally, this would be an empty promise. Beware! She would definitely make a comeback again and again.

'HANTU TETEK'

Living in a village environment is fun. We have acres of land to run around in and many friends to play with. We also have the beaches and the sea to swim in or catch fish in freely. When the tide was coming in we would go fishing. During the low tide, we could catch mollusc sea snails, and our favorite the flower crab.

The flower crab would hide under the sea bed. So as we walked bare footed in ankle to knee-deep water, and with some experience, we could feel the crab's hard shell under our sole. We would then slowly catch them from their backs with our bare hands—this was really fun though. Occassionally we got pinched by it. Another way of catching the flower crab is by using a spear. This needs real skill, as the crab is very elusive and hard to find in the water.

To catch the mollusc another kind of skill is needed. Besides scraping the sand we needed to have sharp eyes to notice bubbles or smoky like substances coming out from the sea bed. We'd dig there, a big mollusc was always to be found.

The houses in the village where I live are made of woods and attaps/zinc roof. Some of the houses are made on four feet stilts. Some are totally on the ground with half bricks and half wood. Normally, the toilet would be about fifteen to twenty meters away from the house, while the bathroom where the well was, would be about ten meters away from the kitchen. The makeshift bathrooms were made of wood, zinc and sometimes with only coconuts leaves as for the wall. It's really inconvenient, especially if you had a stomach ache at night.

When such a thing happened, I would wake up my elder brother or sister to accompany me. It's pitch dark at night, and we depended on the torch to walk to the toilet. Frightening? Yes! A bit but, we got all used to it.

There are several acres of land for each of them. Behind the land would be another family property and their house. Some of the properties are left vacant or abandoned by the owner. In this land, they would normally plant some fruits trees or vegetables. Fruits are abundant, and there are many kinds of them throughout the year. Some of the villagers were also rearing poultry.

On one of these fruits plantations lived a very beautiful young girl, probably sweet seventeen. We used to play truant behind her house where there was an orchard. The family didn't mind we plucked some of the 'rambutan'.

One day near to sunset we happened to be on top of one of the 'rambutan' tree and saw the beauty come out of the makeshift bathroom. She was clad only in her 'sarong batik' (batik loin cloth) from the chest to her knees. She didn't notice us.

She was drying hair with another piece of a towel. She looked so beautiful under the light from the fifteen-watts bulb which was hanging at the bathroom's entrance. We developed the desire to peep at the lady while she was bathing one day. It was Joe's idea. Though the spectacle was not that clear, her action was enough to arouse both of us. The next day we went there much earlier. We climbed up to one of the 'rambutan' trees which was about ten meters away from the bathroom. We sat quietly on top of the branch for more than half an hour when the lady came out. We were so excited.

However, from that angle and height, what we could see was her hand washing her hair. We could not see the rest of the body. It was not so clear as it was quite a distance away, and then the bathroom, which had no roof was lighted by a 15 watts bulb. We just remained auietly until the lady finish her toilet. We started to make a better plan for the following day. We intended to go right to the zinc wall of the makeshift toilet. There were some bushes there for us to hide.

For the first time in our lives watching a sweet seventeen naked body, we were very excited. Both of us looked at each other and giggled. Then we realized how stupid we were. We put our index finger on our lips as a sign to keep quiet. When we tried to look at the hole again the young lady threw a bucket of water towards the hole. We realized that she sensed that someone was watching her bathing. We got up quickly and ran away. When we were far enough away we stopped, to catch a breathe. We giggled all the way home. There were no words to describe what we saw, and the feeling at that moment.

The following afternoon after school, both of us roamed the village as if nothing had happening the previous night. However, when we are passing by the big bosom sweet seventeen's house, we started to whisper and giggle. You surely know what we were giggling about. Suddenly, she called us by our names (she knew us well) sweetly. She asked nicely if we could help her go to the shop and buy some groceries for her. This was not the first times she had asked us. The shop was only about a kilometer away. It wouldn't be a problem at all. We approached her happily, not feeling guilty and suspicious at all.

As we came closed enough, she put her left hand in her pocket as if searching for money. As fast as lightning, five cents landed on my right cheek. Ping! I saw a sparkling star. I never expected her to give me such a hard slap. However, before another one landed on my left cheek, I had turned and ran away. Joe was caught with a surprise too. He stood still like a stupid statue.

The young lady caught one of his hands and try to give him a nice slap. He managed to block it a few times. The lady got a better idea. She pinched his breast. He was screaming in pain. All he could do was to hold her fist and ask for mercy.

'Enough Sister! Enough Sister!' He shouted, 'Aw! Aw!'

The beauty showed no mercy turning her hand left and right, and Joe had to follow her hand movement to avoid the extreme pain. He would have retaliated strongly if she had been a boy.

The commotion attracted the attention of the fat old lady, her mother in the house. She stood by the window and scolded her daughter and asked her to let Joe go.

'This is the Peeping Tom, Ma! This is the Peeping Tom Ma!'

'Ok, let him go, I said!'

As she was turning and answering her mother, the pinch got to loosen a bit, and Joe managed to escape and ran off. He saw me waiting about fifty metres down the road. We proceeded to our secret hide out.

He was still rubbing his breast in pain when we reach our tree house at the back of my house. I saw a bit of blood on his T-shirt.

'Hey! Got blood.'

'Where?'

I pointed at his T-shirt. He wiped it off, and we could see that she was on target; she had pinched his right nipple until bleedings.

'Why didn't you give her a push?'

'I felt guilty about hitting a young and beautiful girl. Wouldn't You?'

'You! You're right. I felt the same.'

'You cheek is reddish and swollen.'

'Oh! Really.'

I felt my right cheek. I could feel it was a bit hot, with three branch bulging lines across it. She must have given me a hard slap.

'Eh! Now! How?' She knew it was both of us who peeped at her last night.

Joe sounds worried, 'Well what should we do?'

'Just wait and see for the punishment.'

We spent the whole afternoon in a secret place. In the evening we went home. I was greeted with a good scolding by my mother. Later when my father came home, I expected a beating from him—fortunately, he just gave me another good scolding.

In the morning, I found out that Joe, who stayed a few houses away from mine got a good beating from his stepmother. His real mother had left the village after discovering that his father had a mistress. She asked for divorced and left the village. At that time Joe was barely eight years old. His father remarried a few years later. As usual, the step mother lived up to her expectation as cruel—she never loved Joe and ill treated him without his father's knowledge.

By now, the whole village found out the story of the two of us. We were quickly nicknamed 'Peeping Toms'. It was very embarrassing to carry this title with us to wherever we went. Fortunately, it lasted for about six months only. The incident had shaken the whole village.

A four-year toddler boy was missing. He was supposed to be playing with his elder sister who was two years older than him at the family hall. The father was away for work. The mother, a full time housewife, was busy in the kitchen. She discovered her son was missing at about nine in the morning when her daughter came running to the kitchen and told her that her brother was taken away by a scary granny.

'Gone with who?'

'Granny! A naked granny!'

The mother went up to the hall followed by her daughter. She called out his name loudly and searched the whole house. She also went down to check under her house and in the surrounding compound. She couldn't find him.

'Which way did he go?'

'I don`t know. Just now the scary granny came and took him away.' She started to cry.

'Which way did they go?'

'They flew away and disappeared.' She pointed to the door.

The mother went to her neighbor`s house to ask them whether they had seen her son wandering around. None of them had noticed her son. She became panickly and telephone her husband. Meanwhile, news had already spread throughout the village about the missing toddler.

Attentions was now focused on searching for the toddler. Her husband came home in the afternoon with his 'Bomoh' (faith healer) friend who after performing some ritual, claimed that the toddler was kidnapped by a Breast Ghost. He was still alive and would be returned only twenty-four hours later. He told them not to worry. He foresaw that the toddler would be sent home the following morning.

Which parent would not be worried, and would have stopped searching when such a thing had happened? Which parent would stop worrying? The parent and the villagers would not give up either. A Police report was also made by the father. A Police search party with some

Rangers and villagers began to comb the whole village thoroughly until late at night—to no avail.

Sure enough, the next morning the little toddler was found by a group of anglers who were on their way back from night fishing, They happened to walk under a wax apple tree near an old cemetery about five hundred meters from the toddler's home. He was found engrossed in playing with loose sand and some wax apples he had gathered. Strangely, that area had been searched a few times yesterday, and there was no sign of him. The brave toddler didn't cry. He wasn't hungry or thirsty.

The anglers heard about the missing toddler, so they carried him with them. The parents were so delighted that their only son had been recovered. The whole village now forgot about the Peeping Tom and was busy spreading the news about the Breast Ghost and how the toddler had been mystically found in the morning.

I and Joe were relieved. At least, the villagers were slowly forgetting about us the Peeping Tom and the mischief that we had done. Life carried on as usual. We were now having freer times as it was December and the school holidays had just begun. Our parents wouldn't let us wander too freely. We were enrolled to attend tuition classes during the some days, and religious classes at night twice a week.

We had to pass by the Big Bosom lady's house every time we were going or coming back from the classes. Sometimes during the day we would purposely pass by the lady's house just to take a glimpse of her. She pretended not to notice us. Whenever we were walking or cycling in front of her house, we're hoping that she would asked us for a favour. Perhaps she also felt some kind of embarrassment, and didn't want to get close to us. We have no chance to said that we're sorry. Perhaps sorry no cure for both of us.

Once in a while we saw the sweet seventeen going in and out of the bathroom. Somehow that triggered our desire to plan another attempt to peep at her as we had missed it so much.

'You are not scared?' I asked.

'Scared of what?'

'The Breast Ghost.'

'Which Breast Ghost, the one in front of us, Oh! I love her,' Joe said jokingly. He knew what I meant.

'The real Breast Ghost would only kidnap toddlers—you see there is no harm done to that little boy after all.'

I had nothing to say but agreed with Joe, who is two years older than me. I was only thirteen. Actually, during the day, we were making discreet surveys of the area again. The bushes beside and behind the bathroom had grown even taller now and bushier now. We were planning to approach the bathroom just like the last time. I couldn't believed it.

We had learnt from our mistake. Furthermore she would have forgotten about the incident, and would never expect a return. So without further delay, that very evening as the sun was setting, we went right to the wall of the makeshift bathroom quietly and were careful enough not to make the slightest noise. We didn't even dare to hit the mosquitoes, just rubbing our hands to avoid any noise.

After waiting for a long fifteen minutes, the bathroom light was on. The dimly bulb was switched on, and we knew and heard someone was coming. So we took our own position perfect for the best view. Oh! NO! It was the fat old lady, the mother who came. In a jiff, she took off everything. We almost giggled and give ourselves a slip again. We managed to control it. What a perfect view of the fats all around her body. Both of us—we're not turned on at all.

We are not interested to watch the fat old lady bathe. We felt it would be a sin. So, we just sat around hoping for the next show. After the old lady was out, we waited and waited for nearly an hour in the dark with a lot of mosquitoes attacking us, but she didn't turn up. Disappointed, we went back wondering what had happened to the beauty.

Later, we heard gossip that she had gone for a short holiday with her friend for a week with some of her relatives. We were longing for her to come back. Six more nights would be a very long wait. Finally, she was back again. We enjoyed the free shows at least twice a week for about six months without being discovered by anybody.

She had applied to become a teacher and was enrolled at the Teachers Training College. She went to stay with her auntie who was staying near the college. She would come back occasionally, but we're unable to track her routine. We had to give up on her. We combed the whole vilage in search for another Breast Ghost, but we couldn't find any to replace her.

Had the Beast Ghost struck again? This time my very best friend, my buddy for years was the victim—my Joe. He was found missing without a trace. I remembered he told me that the Breast Ghost only went after toddlers. Why he was missing now? Some speculated that his stepmother had silenced him and buried him somewhere in the orchard ground behind the house.

As usual, police reports were made, and a search party was organized. 'Bomohs' were also called in. After a week of tireless effort, he was still not to be found. Everybody became so tired and bored, and the search slowly died off naturally. I became very sad and lonely now while other villagers had easily forgotten about my dear Joe. I had no more friends to wonder around the village. A good friend like Joe was hard to find.

I concentrated on my study and stayed at home most of the time. I had many other friends in the village. However, no one could replace Joe. His stepmother was the happiest woman on earth as she had escaped from taking care of the mischievous Joe. However, his father became very remorseful.

Two years later I received a letter from across the causeway. I was so excited as I didn't have any contact there, who could it be? I was so happy that I didn't realize tears drop down from my eyes. It was from Joe. He told me he was fine and was following his mother going north. It was sad that I wouldn't be able to communicate with him further as he didn't give his return address. Joe asked me to keep this a secret, especially from his stepmother.

A few days later by chance I met his father fishing at the beach looked lifeless and still remorseful. I make him to promise me not to tell his wife if I were to tell him this secret. I told him even my own parent didn't know about this. He agreed. When I told him that Joe was still alive and now following his mother going north.

He was so happy that he couldn't control his tears. He grabbed me for long seconds, so hard as if I was his missing son. Joe's father turned to his normal self instantly. He was very much alive after hearing the great news. He didn't mind Joe following his mother as long as he was alive and fine.

In 2010, I met Joe when I went for a holiday in Penang. I still could recognized him though this was thirty years later. The birth mark on his right jaw, below the right ear was still very prominent. Guess what was the first question he asked me?

'How is the Breast Ghost?'

'You are horrible! After so long of separation, instead of asking about my well-being, or how your father is, you ask about that ghost.'

'Sorry! Sorry! Anyway don't tell me you have forgotten about her.'

'Ok Lah! For your information, she is a grandmother of two now.'

'That man is very lucky.' Joe showed a little of his feeling.

'Are you sure? Do you remember her mother, the fat lady?'

'That fat lady. Yes! Of course.'

'She looked exactly like that.'

'So fat?' Joe was grinning.

'How! Still interested? Her husband passed away few years ago.'

Joe was stunned. I knew he was engrossed in his memory lane in his mind right then. The moment that we had watch the free show was still fresh.

'Anyway, if you want to know how your wife would look like when she is old. Take a good look at your mother-in-law right now.'

We have so much thing to catch up, so many things to tell each other. Bye!

BEING FOLLOWED

A lot of men in Singapore smoke. The majority of them are not allowed to smoke in the house at all. Especially those who are married and have littlechildren at home. During the courting period the young lady is more understanding and would tolerate this bad habit. However, once married and living with the man she loved under the same roof, she would find that the secondary smoking from the cigarettes really irritating. It`s a real nuisance.

Hisham, who is married with two children is no different. He and his family are living in a high-rise public housing estate. They lived on the 4th floor. Once married his wife opposed him smoking strongly. They had many arguments and she tried all kinds of ways, like hiding his lighter and cigarettes to try to get him to stop smoking, but to no avail.

One night after dinner, as usual, Hisham would puff at the living room while watching TV. His wife came and lighted a cigarette too. Hisham watched with much amusement. Then, she lighted another one. Now! he looked at her with a surprised. She placed both lighted cigarettes together and put it to her delicate lips to smoke. One puff! only. She was coughing and coughing for a few minutes.

There was nothing much he could do except to take away the cigarettes from her fingers which she allowed willingly and gave her a teasing smile. From that day onwards she never argued about him smoking in the house. She would go into the bedroom and shut the door to avoid the secondary smoke.

When they got a little one, the wife brought up the issue again. He fought for what he thought it was his right to smoke. His wife finally gave up. 'But, at least don't hurt me and your little ones with the secondary smoke from your cigarette. Please smoke outside the house. Do not harm your innocent little baby.'

The wife pleaded seriously. He compromised. So no choice, whenever he craved for a puff, he would go out of the house to the building's corridor at certain time of midnight.

Sometimes the neighbors who passed by would make a gesture like coughing or fanning their face as a sign of displeasure. Some who knew him well, would tell him off boldly:

'Don't smoke laah, smelly laa!' a neighor said;

'You don't love your health!' another one said;

'If you got so much money, don't burn away your money,' a kind old man said;

'You are so clever, why don't you smoke inside your own apartment?' A scarstic neighbor passes remaks a few times;

'Now! You want to kill your neighbor,' some said angrily, there were many other comments that went through his right ear and came out through his left ear. Despite all these, he still craved for cigarettes and continued to smoke freely.

One night he was awakened about one in the morning. After taking some tap water and easing himself, he felt like smoking. He took his packet of cigarette and lighter and went out to his favorite smoking spot. It was very cool and refreshing out there. The surrounding area was quiet and serene. He had been enjoying his cigarette at this hour for the past few year already. He would puff his cigarette, looked around, enjoy the scenery and the cool breeze before he went to bed.

About forty meters away in front of his apartment was another apartment block. Car parks and some trees separated the two blocks. He smiles in his heart to see that at this wee hour of the morning, there were still people just come back from work or from wherever they did outsides, yet at the same time there were people who were living their apartment for whatever business they might have.

He watched a taxi come into the car park and stop near the lobby of the opposite block. He saw a young girl come out of the taxi. Another lady followed her from behind. The lady who followed her acted very strangely. She had a long dark hair almost touching the ground and piece of white cloth covering her body. He got excited and lit up another stick.

He kept watching them closely, almost not blinking. The girl stopped, rubbed her neck and shoulder and walked on. May be she got goose pimples. A few steps later she stopped and turned around. the lady behind her would stop when she stopped and continued to follow her when she walked on. She went up the stairs to the first floor and walk along the corridor. She stopped a few more times. Hisham believed she didn't see anything behind her. She looked nervous and her stride was longer and faster now. She reached for her shoulder bag and took out the house key; hurriedly she opened the door and went in. She closed the door behind her.

Perhaps she felt safe and relieved after entering her apartment. At that moment, the lady who followed her was standing in front of her door, like a statue, for some time, and suddenly disappeared. Hisham became more excited and wondered where that being could have gone to. By now, he knew what he thought was correct. Surely that was not a human being.

With his eyes opened widely, he combed the corridor, the car park and even the trees. He still couldn't find her. He scanned another time more thoroughly; he still couldn't find her, and he was not satified. The ash on his cigarette was getting longer as he didn't puff it while watching the drama.

He shook it and took a puff. He sensed that there was something in the left-hand corner of his own corridor, moving slowly towards him, shuffling slippers, which created a sweeping sound. He turned and took a good look and knew that this was the same lady in white whom he had been searching for. He could see her clearly under the corridor light. Confirmed!

This was the lady who had followed his neighbor earlier. He tried to pretend as if nothing had happened and continued to puff even when his goose pimples were rising. He heard a high pitched trembling voice calling his name, greeting him softly.

'Hello! Hisham . . . Is it me you're looking for?

He turned around and saw that the lady ghost was much nearer now; It was about five meters away only. Without delay, he threw away the cigarette, stepped on it with his slippers and walked back to his home without looking back. He locked the door properly and went to sleep. If you were Hisham what would you have done?

After that night, somehow he felt a little nervous and dared not to go out to his favourite spot as usual to smoke after dinner. He was also very wary, his eyes looked around wildly whenever he came home late from work. The frightened Hisham never told his wife about the incident. He didn't wish his wife to become worried unnecessarily. Sometimes it's better not to know.

Whenever we came home late at night, we never knew who would be following us home from behind. Only those people with the third eyes would be able to see them. Often by chance, an ordinary person like Hisham, you and me would be able to see them also. A one time experience is enough to be remembered for life.

It was fortunate for that girl not to see what was following her from behind that night. If she had seen it I wonder what would have happened to her? Maybe she would have screamed, cried or fainted. The worst that could have happened is that she could have gone to hysteria. In other words, she could have been possessed.

Hisham managed to cut back one or two cigarettes a day. At times he became more conscious and uncomfortable when he got to puff outside the office when he was the only one standing at a lonely staircases and smoking for a few minutes there. He always imagine that the lady might come onto the landing where he used to puff and frighten him again—who know if he might get heart attack.

Finally, he gave up smoking totally. The happiest person would be his wife, though she did't know the real reason why her beloved husband had stopped smoking.

GHOST AT SEA

When I told my cousin about my intention to write a ghost story book, he encouraged me. He even related to me some stories about his experiences and stories that he had heard from his circle of friends. Most of the stories are similar, which is about the presence of the beings in the house, sightings, and the screaming of the 'Pontianak' at the park, stories I've heard off.

Nevertheles, there is one story which is entirely different. It was his own experienced and it happened at sea. This is what he told me in his own words . . .

You know I liked fishing very much, right? Almost every weekend when I was not working I would go fishing, sometimes alone. Most of the time I would go with a group of friends. When

I said fishing you surely imagine the fishing line and the fishing gear like reels, rods, hooks and all that. No! My method of fishing is different. I throw a casting net, so did all my group of friends.

In this method of fishing one had to walk in the sea up to waist level or a little deeper to throw a specially made casting net. Properly thrown, the net will open in a wide circle on the surface of the sea. The uniquely shaped lead weight would sink and brought the net down smoothly. Any fish within this circle radius will be trapped.

Then you have to pull the net together slowly. While pulling the net you could feel the net vibrate as the fish rammed into the net trying to escape. Here is the best part. As you are pulling you can guess what type of fish was trapped in the net now. Over time, your guessing gets really accurate The caught fish would be kept in the floating styrofoam box. Some brought along a narrow-mouthed basket for holding freshly caught fish.

I remembered when I joined this group I was extremely excited. I remebered the first time I followed them to go catch fish at night, I was told that it would be more interesting and always a good catch. We chartered a bump boat and shared the cost equally. At about 6 pm, we proceeded on a calm water to an island, Pulau Hantu—literally mean Ghost Island, which is about twenty minutes away from Singapore, by the bumboat.

When we reached the destination, the bumboat operator left and promised to come back to fetch us in the next morning at 7 am. The tide was still high, so we walked slowly to the favourite fishing spot. Two men erected a small camp to keep our belongings. We sat by the beach talking and smoking peacefully. It was almost at around 10 pm that the tide started to go down. When it was low enough the leader got up and said, 'Let's go.'

For the first time I went into the sea at night. You'd be suprised that the water isn't cold at all. In fact it is very warm and comfortable. We walked Into the sea up to waist level, those with more experience went in slightly deeper water or rather slightly above their waists to throw the casting net. Strangely, after casting for about an hour, I didn't catch any fish nor did the others. Out of the quietness of the night, the leader sang,

'Here she come, with her sweet fragrance, she means no harm, just doesn't like our presence.'

He repeated it many times and started to move to the shore, followed by the rest, including myself, though I didn't know what was happening. However, when the water was knee-deep, I stopped and started to throw my casting net, still hoping to get something while the rest of them proceeded to the shore.

There was no one else at the sea except me at that time. I turned around, and under the bright moon light, I saw all of them; they were relaxing, some with cigarett enjoying the night. I was pulling in my net when I saw a dark toddler clearly crawling through my net, I was stunned. It's dissappeared as fast as it had appeared.

I was looking around, searching for it when suddenly, I felt someone grab me from behind. I shouted, screamed and struggled. 'Let me go!' At the same time I heard the laughter of my gang on the shore. Quickly, I pulled the casting net and proceeded to join them, shivering from the cold wind on the beach and the shock earlier. I felt hurt, instead of helping me they were all laughing at me hilariously. But, may be there were talking among themselves and laughing while somebody was telling jokes.

When I reach the camp, they laughed at me once again while the leader asked,

'Why didn't you comes in with us?'

Before I make an effort to answer him, he said,

'Earlier you saw a dark toddler crawling through your casting net, right! Then something was grabbing you from behind, right!'

I was pleased that someone had set up a camp fire. Otherwise I would continued to shiver.

I nodded in agreement. He continued to explain to me that this kind of experience always happened to the new comer. It meant no harm. It`s just a warning that it doesn`t like our presence. That was just two of them, they`re plenty more. That`s why we all moved out of the water. We had to wait until the fragrance was gone before we could go down and continue to cast; hopefully we would get a good catch tonight. Everybody laughed.

'Most importantly don`t boast that you`re are not afraid of them. Don`t under estimate or try to challenge them.'

He told me he lost a close friend a few years ago.

'How did it appened?' I asked anxiously.

'We were sitting around around the camp fire, just like we`re doing now when my friend saw a beautiful girl walk by the beach at the edge of the water. My friend said, "Oh! Guys, what a beauty! Let me go and catch her!" We tried to stop him as we dnd he himself knew that it wasn`t a human being. There was nobody staying on this Island. Furthermore it`s just not right that a young girl would be walking along the beach, alone in the middle of the night like this. Instead he said we were cowards and he would show us that he would bring the girls back. He chased after her. The faster he ran, the faster she moved. Finally she turned towards the sea, and he followed. This was when we all panicked shouting and running after him to stop him from following her. It was too late; he dived into the sea, he was a good swimmer and swam towards her and was submerged—missing, the figure also dissappeared right in front of our eyes. His body was found floating face down by the Marine Police diver in the afternoon at the same spot where we last saw him. The area had been searched a few times since morning.'

There was a solemn moment for a while before the leader continued his story.

'Here's a piece of advice from me. Please do not stare too long at empty spaces, trees, any strange things or figure or anything, alright?' Urged the leader.'

'OK, I understand.' I answered shyly.

While we were talking, the sweet fragrance still lingered around us a while. According to him that's the sign the being is still around, and we have to wait patiently until it's totally gone before we could go into the water again.

'Normally, they only come once. Perhaps this is their hunting ground also. Once it's gone it's our turn to fish.'

The sweet fragrance was finally gone. We went down into the sea again. We started to throw our casting net, and all of us had a very good catch. We caught a lot of big fish like the sea bass, red fish and grouper. When the tide was coming in, the sea level became too high for us to cast our net. We went back to the shore, dead tired. It was four in the morning. We fell asleep until the bum boat operator came to fetched us at about seven in the morning, as promised.

My cousin got hooked, and still continue to fish with the same gang. He invited me a few times.

'Me! Follow you fishing at night? No! No! No Way! Not Me! I've got to admit, I'm a little coward. I don't know what I would do if I were to experience what you had experienced.'

GHOST  HUNTERS

The historic Changi Hospital building stands proudly on top of a solid hill, in the most eastern part of Singapore. This is one of the greatest and most widely reported haunted sites. The gloomy sight of it`s surounding with many tall trees that are more than a hundred years old is enough to send shivers of trepidation down anyone`s spine. However, it`s very inviting to the brave ghost hunters here in Singapore. The surrounding area is lighted dimly, but not the building itself. Can you imagine the gloomy look of the old building?

The Hospital building was constructed in 1930 by the British. It was abandonedp in 1997, ever since a new and modern hospital was ready and started functioning a few kilometres away. Many stories have been told by the staff, patients, taxi drivers and visitors of sighting of spirits of many races and kinds wondering around inside and outside the hospital compound. It is widely known, and everyone knew about it. Simply mentioning the name would have made some people feel uncomfortable.

When the Japanese landed in February 1942, OCH was converted to a military hospital where all the wounded soldiers and civilians were treated. After the Japanese left in 1945, it was converted back to a public hospital.

In February 1997, OCH was closed as it was being replaced by the new Changi General Hospital, a few kilometers away. Ever Since it was left vacant, the OCH became even more isolated. Perhaps it has become heaven for those wandering spirits. It's given an eerie feeling to whoever passes near by the area, even during the day, especially if you are alone.

The stories about the building being haunted started even during the Japanese Occupation. The Hospital had witnessed much brutal torture and suffering that took place during the Japanise Occupation. Until today, the ghostly experience, like the ugly figures, human-like figures, floating orbs, flying white cloth, clinking sound of iron, and serious temperature drops still linger around in the hospital. The least one could experience is a sweet scent of the frangipani flower (remember this is a warning sign of their presence, and that you have intruded into their territory, and that they may not like it)

No wonder this place had become the number one spot for ghost hunters here in Singapore. It was so popular that almost every weekend, there will be several explorers visiting the place at night hoping to get some chilling experience. It's still said that the dark mysterious figures really roam the empty hospital. Some believe that it is the souls of those that once suffered, and died on the hospital bed there. Others believe its some ghosts that made the place their supposed sanctuary and multiplied. They are still lingering in the empty ward rooms.

The best experience you could get is if you visit the place with few friends only. Too many people in a group would send the ghost hiding behind the door, window or on the ceiling watching your every movement. Going alone is even better if you have the guts, but it's not recommended at all as nobody can assist you if you are in trouble. This is real; you'll never find yourself alone though. I guaranteed that you would find some chill experience. A big reminder! If you are thinking about investigating this place, it is considered trespassing. You are not only unwelcome by the owner of the place in this case, the Singapore Government. But, also those spirits that have made this place their home and playground. Acquiring prior permission would be wise but who will grant you permission, unless you have a special reason.

Many who have been there and some spooky feeling always comes back with an almost identical description of their experience. The most common one would be to feel a gush of cold wind passing, followed by a drop in temperature. A sweet scent that you never smelt before, and the stench smell. These are enough to make all your hair stand up on end. A lady figure in white with long hair is another common sight.

Normally, a loud bang of the door and windows being opened and closed with a squeaking sound would give you some reasons to be frightened. Finally, if you are still brave enough, a long deafening scream Haa! Haa! Haa! Haaa! Haa! Haa! It would surely send you running for your life.

This is where many would get injured or faint as they were dashing about in the dark looking for the exit. I was made to understand that if the screaming was very loud and deafening, it meant that the spirit was probably at a distance or about to leave the place. That could be its last attempt to frighten you off. If you were brave enough they were the one who would leave, but don't take chances. However, if the screaming was soft and sounded as if it was far away, you'd better be careful. The spirit was very near or probably just moved in closer to you. You may even get possessed by it. Anyway, many of the victims were womenfolk.

Nevertheless, here is one story that I would like to share. There was this group of motor cyclists (three man and two young ladies) who after roaming around the island one Saturday night, landed themselves at the hospital compound illegally, in other words by trespassing. Normally, there would be a security guard at that place. On that day, there was none. Many of the security guards are reluctant to be attached to OCH. The brave ones would definitely encounter the spirits. Actually these motorcyclists ended up here on the suggestion of one of the girls in the group, Noraini. They reluctantly followed her wishes after she challenged hem as cowards. Would the ghosts of Changi Hospital come out to welcome or frightened them tonight?

They were all not well prepared as this plan was an imprompt one. The least they should have had was some good torch lights, but none of them had them. Even so, they decided to steel themselves to go into the pitch-dark building, using only the light from their mobile phones.

Just, a few step into the building they were already welcomed by the sweet scent, a sign the presence of the unseen. All of them knew about the sign and kept quiet. A few more steps into the building, and they could hardly move as the light from their phones was very limited. Suddenly, just a few meters in front of them appeared from nowhere a floating white cloth.

They got a shock and screamed. They turned around to the exit and ran for their lives, except Noraini. When they reached the place where they had parked their motor-cycles, they were out of breath. They realized that Noraini was not with them. After some hesitation, they had no choice but to go back into the building to find her. They walked closely to each other. Slowly, step by step, they entered the building again.

There was an unpleasant smell this time. They found Noraini standing like a statue near a window. Two of the boys grabbed her by the hand and told her,

'Let's leave this place.'

She answered in the coarse voice of an old lady, 'Go where? This is my home.'

Ignoring the strange voice from Noraini, they tried to pull her— she didn't budge an inch. One of them tried to carry her. She was too heavy for him. Two of them tried this time still they were unable to lift her off the ground.

Suddenly, she screamed loudly,

'Haaa Haaaa haaa haaa haaa haaaa haaaa hee hee hee hee hee!' in a deafening high-pitched tone. They don't know what to do. Filled with panic and scared, they ran out of the building a second time. They left her alone a second time. They walked to the main road which is about 50 meters away, and they tried to hail some passing motorists, but many ignored them. Some seemed not to notice them at all.

It was past midnight, and it was a long wait for another car to pass by. A taxi stopped, but after hearing the problem, he sped off. The second taxi did the same—those taxi drivers were just too afraid to get involve. The third taxi driven by an old Malay man stopped and readily drove them back to the location.

They led him to whe Noraini had been left earlier. Surprisingly, she was still stood there like a statue. Her head was shaking left and right wildly—she was in trance. The old man said that Noraini was being possessed. He stood right in front of her and asked her why she possessed this girl. In a hard coarse voice, she said,

'They came and disturbed me!'

'Forgive them and leave her alone,' begged the taxi driver.

'No! I want her I want her she's mine.'

'You have no right over her body.'

There was an extreme silence for a moment, and still no answer.

'You have to leave her body.' There's no answer.

'You leave, or I'll do it the hard way.'

The hard way is that he was going to recite some verses from the Quran, which was believed to cause it to be in great pain. The negotiation took quite some time as the taxi driver kept repeating the same question again and again. The taxi driver recited something into Noraini's right ear. Finally, the angry spirit agreed to leave.

'I'll leave now, but will surely come back again later, haa haaa haaa haaa heee hee hee hee!' The deafening sound was the loudest they had all ever heard in their lives.

Noraini recovered and was in a daze. She couldn't remember what had happened. They brought her out of the building. The taxi drivers instructed them to leave the place immediately and advised them to get further treatment from spiritual healers. They begged the taxi driver for help to send her home. Seeing her condition he kindly agreed. They went straight to her apartment where her parents who had been informed by phone about the incident were waiting at the ground floor.

Noraini was never the same again. Though her parents brought her for treatment to many faith healers, she never got back to her normal self. Psychiatric treatment could not cure her. They classified her as having a mental breakdown. The parents refused further treatment from the hospital. They didn't like the idea that Noraini was to be warded in a Mental Hospital. So, they brought her home.

The parents didn't give up that easily and welcomed a lot of spiritual healers recommended by relatives and friends. Nevertheless, there was no cure. The longest she was normal was about a week. After that she was like a zombie again.

At home, she always isolated herself in the bedroom and was talking to her own self; humming, laughing and at times crying. She always sat in front of a mirror and combed her hair, as if she had long hair right to the waist. She hardly wanted to eat anything and finally, a few months later she passed away at a very young age.

This type of sickness is almost incurable. The fact is they were searching for the ghost. They intruded into the forbidden zone. When it really appeared in its true form, the brains just couldn't take it, and went hay wire. Can we blame the ghost when this kind of thing happens when we're the ones that are so itchy to go out and find them?

Is it worth taking the risk/chances going to such places? We never know if we might offend the unseen forces just by intruding into their hideout. A worse mistake could make is to be boastfu or too brave. Challenging the spirits is not the right thing to do. If you don't believe in them, that's your right, keep it to yourself. It is better to leave them alone. Do not underestimate them.

After all, there are many other interesting places in this world where we can enjoy ourselves.

GHOST  TOUR

The night Ghost Tour was organized by a group of ghost hunters. A bigger bus was hired as there were about forty thrillers eagerly joining the tour this time. Young and old enthusiastic people, but strangely the majorities were women, seeking thrilling night. It seems that women are more interested to find the unseen than the men.

The leader of the group was slightly older than a middle-aged man, sporting himself with a very white 'kurtas' and wearing a white snow hat. He looked like he belonged to Al-Qaedah with his long nose, long beard and thick moustache. However, he was very far away from one, he was not, and would never ever be one he said firmly when he first introduced himself.

He announced that our first destination will be the cemetery area. Singapore is the only place in the world where the burial ground of various races and religions are situated next to each other in a designated area. There are Chinese, Muslim, Hindoos, Christian, Sikh, Persian and many other races in this particular cemetery. I couldn't believe it, they are still neighbors even after their death. In the beginning, there were many cemeteries scattered all over the Island. Almost all had given way to the development as Singapore is a land scares country. If not because many other religion chose cremation, the whole of Singapore Island would be the graveyard.

On arriving, the bus moved more slowly. Everybody was casting their eyes anxiously on the cemetery ground hoping to see something strange or spooky, something that they had never seen or heard before. They had paid and prepared for a chilling experience—to be frightened. As the bus crawled slowly through the quiet and serene cemeteries, they became more anxious, but so far nothing strange had happened.

The driver stopped the bus deep in the middle of the cemetery area and turned off the engine. The participants breathed deeply and heavily. The participants were allowed to get off the bus for fifteen minutes and were advised not to wonder too far away.

However, when the light was off, there was total darkness and a little uneasiness among them. A small scream could be heard here and there in the bus. The leader asked them to keep quiet.

No one was interested in getting off the bus except some men who took the opportunity to have a puff. The participants started to feel restless as there was nothing strange happening except the extreme quietness of the night where they could hear the sound of toads croaking, cricket singing and, once in a while, dogs howling.

Their eyeballs were almost out of their sockets as they looked out anxiously through the bus windows. Under the dimly moonlight, they could only see the shape of the grave like many little hills as they were staring hard into the darkness. After about fifteen minutes, still nothing happened and the leader announced we're moving on to the Japanese Cemetery.

The bus was reaching the exit when the driver did a sudden emergency brake. Some screamed while some chicken hearted ladies started to cry and wondered what was going on. The driver said, 'Sorry! Sorry! Calm down,' the driver calmed them down saying that he was trying to avoid hitting a dog. The panic situation now turned into laughter. After the leader had ensured that everybody was safe, the driver continued the journey to the well known haunted Japanese Cemetery in Singapore. It was about half an hour's drive away as there was no traffic at midnight.

'This place is known to have had some sightings in the past when the area was still undeveloped. The people living in that area used to report being chased by a Japanese soldier in complete army uniform wielding his Samurai Sword. Bus drivers who were driving the last bus scheduled to pass around the area at midnight always became the victim. In the beginning, they were scared when the Japanese soldier appeared right in the middle of the road from nowhere charging directly at them. They got used to it and ignored it.

Since then the surrounding areas had been developed into a private housing estate. Not many sightings were reported. However, it had been reported that there were plenty of orbs in that area; we were lucky if we would be able to see them tonight,' explained the leader while the participants listen anxiously. Within half an hour, they were already near the Old Japanese Cemetery gate where all of them were dropped off. The area was not as eerie as the local cemetery earlier. The surrounding area was bright. There were many street lightsfor the housing estates around the area. As they marched slowly towards the gate, most of the participants witnessed the orbs. There are so many of them, big and small, floating and swaying around and behind the main gate.

The fast workers hurriedly took out their cameras and hand phone sets and took as many quick snaps with their digital cameras. Later when they checked, the orbs were not very clear. They were clearer taken by those experienced photographers as no flash was used in night vision mode. For those using digital cameras with auto flash, the vision is not that clear.

Strangely, there are some participants who didn't see this phenomenon at all, and kept asking desperately, 'What? Where? Show me, show me.' As they got nearer and nearer to the grave area, the orbs disappeared just like flying saucers. Perhaps it was because of the flash lights and noises made by them. The sighting of the orbs was most satisfying to many of them. They lingered around the gate for almost half an hour when the promoter once again announced that they were moving to the next location.

It was nearly three in the morning when they arrive at Punggol area. Matilda House is one of the oldest known most haunted houses in Singapore. It was originally built in 1902. Rumors had it that the uninhabited house is haunted. Therefore, nobody is staying there. Nobody dared to touch it or pull it down for redevelopment. The truth is Matilda House was finally had to give way to redevelopment in 2012.

On the way in the bus earlier, the leader gave them some tips on how to be prepared and what to expect next. The presence of the unseen can be detected when there is a sweet flower scent, a gush of cold wind, sudden extreme quietness, and finally, the long scream, Haaa! Haaa! Haaa! Haaa! Haaa! Haaa! According to him these are some of the common things that people experienced during past trips.

They were advise that If they experienced something like that, to keep it to themselves first, don't panic and not to utter a word. Another good piece of advice was that—if the sound of the laughter was very loud, deafening and frightening, not panic. This was the sign that the spirit is moving away, or it is a distant away from you.

However, he said if the scream was soft, you'd better be careful. The spirit was nearby, and he may not like your presence. Not everybody could hear what you heard, see what you saw or experience what you're going through. The best thing to do is says some prayers and get closer to your partners or friends and leave the place immediately. It is similar when you heard the dog's howling. Most importantly do not worry as the spirits can never harm a human being.

He stopped talking as soon as the bus reached the small road that led to the Matilda House. They excitedly saw the gloomy structure of The Matilda House in the dark. This was possible now as many trees and bushes at the surrounding area had been cleared. Despite the vigorous development of high rise apartments in the surrounding area, the place still looks eerie.

As the bus entered a small lane, they were welcomed by dogs howling. Everybody was very obliging as no sound was heard from any of them. Though the house was fixed with security lights at all four corners, for safety reasons, it's indeed an eerie scene looking at the only big empty bungalow house made of wood with a zinc roof in the middle of empty grounds.

Explorers had to jump over a small drain and climb up a bank to a higher ground as the bus couldn't go any further. They were lucky the plain was dry as there had been no rain in the last few days; otherwise it would have been quite impossible to walk in a muddy plain for about fifty meters to reach the house.

Everybody obeyed the order to keep silent and not to use torchlight as the beam from the lights of the Matilda House, and the dim moonlight were bright enough for them to advance with a fast thumping heart.

The surrounding area of the Matilda House had been recently fenced, to protect it from being vandalized as well as protecting the enthusiasts from injuring themselves as the house was classified as unsafe for habitation. Suddenly, many shutters from the cameras broke the silence of the night as many witnessed orbs on top of the roof for a few seconds. The orbs came and off, big and smal, moving around the house countless times. Everybody witnessed it.

But again, Orbs! A lot of orbs only appeared in the photos of those experienced photographers as they took the picture with no flash and used the night vision mode.

The house is extremely quiet—it had no voice that night. If it had! Guess what stories it might tell? It could only have screamed with the high-pitched voice of a lady—whose utterance didn't tell whether she was in pain or happy, or maybe teasing you or laughing at you when you got frightened and screamed on top of your voice or cry and start to run head over heels.

Later, many admitted that there was a kind of eerie feeling, chilling, inducing goose pimples standing up all the time when they were near the house. Some participants reported sweating in that very cold night. They spent quite sometimes there, only to feel a kind of relief when the leader finally announced, 'Let's get back to the bus.'

They went around the house for the last time before heading back to the bus. Many were satisfied with the experience of the night, and showed interest to join the group again in the next adventure. They are many more places here that are classified as haunted, spooky and very active with the strong negative energy.

Among those worth mentioning are in the pipeline for the next visit:

The Kranji old Cemetery—This old Muslim Cemetery is more than hundred years old and known to be haunted by the 'Pontianak'.

Kassim Cemetery Ground—This is a private cemetery situated in a gloomy housing estate at Siglap.

Bukit Brown—An old Chinese burial ground which was infested with many types of spirits lingering around the graveyards. At night, it`s totally dark as there are many big trees around. There are no street light the moment you enter into the cemetery ground.

Old Changi Hospital—It has been left vacant since 1997 till this book is published in 2013. Many spooky stories have been experienced by many explorers. A must see.

Changi Coast Beach—One part at the beach where there are a lot of pine trees is known to have a lot of mischievous ghosts who like to frightened anglers or campers who go there at night. Perhaps they don`t like to be disturbed and meant to chase them away only.

Sembawang Park Beach—Here is where a lot of people used to practice their black magic in the past. It has been said that many spirits have been let loose here once they were no longer needed.

WHEN A GHOST SAT ON ME

Here is my true experience of seeing a ghost for the first time in my life. Have you ever seen one? At least, I'm sure everybody would have an experience or sensed that something was around staring at us. I was a teenager then, about fifteen years old when I had my first encounter. It happened right in my house, in my own bedroom.

I was at my study table doing my homework as usual. I like to study in the wee hours of the morning when everybody was fast asleep. Normally, it would be around twelve midnights to two in the morning. The environment would be extremely quiet, and I could concentrate better. There was no distraction at all.

On one particular night, I felt a little strange when a gust of chilled wind was suddenly brushing the back of my neck followed by a smell of smooth sweet scent came through the window, which was slightly opened. I turned back and looked around. This confirmed that the bedroom windows were slightly opened. Logically, I thought that the smell must be coming from the flowering trees outside the house.

I was comforting myself by saying that if the ghost were to appear or disturb me, why hadn't it happened yesterday or the day before yesterday or during the last fifteen years. With more courage now, I stood up and walked heavily to shut the windows. I've got to admit that I still feel a little scared.

There was a strong impulse in my heart telling me that this smell is extremely strange. It was extra sweet, and I had never smelt such a sweet scent before in my life. I couldn't remember if there are any flowers around my house having this kind of smell. So this must be the smell of the frangipani flower which was always associated with the presence of the 'Pontianak'. The thought of it alone made goose pimples on the back of my neck and my hand I rubbed my neck and my hand a few times.

From that time, I started to feel as if someone was watching me from behind. I thought my mother was awake, and wanted to make me some hot drink as she always did. However, when I turned around, there was no one around and nothing in the thin air. I could feel that everybody was sleeping soundly as I heard some of them snoring heavily.

I got more frightened now, I switched on the MP3, plugged the ear piece into my ears and sat back to continue with my study. However, the feeling of someone lingering and looking at me from behind kept haunting me. I couldn't concentrate, and kept recalling the smell I sensed earlier. I admitted in my heart that I was really scared, and decided to switch off the light and go to bed in the bunk which was beside my study table. I guess I was just too tired.

The feelings of being watched bothered me. I became restless, turning left and right—right and left. I don't know for how long I'd been trying to sleep. Every time, I felt my eyes heavily about to close, I was awakened time and again by a jerk at certain parts of my body. At times, I felt like I was falling from a high place and woke up.

Finally, I started to have sleeping paralysis. There was this uneasy buzzing sound that came and went for some time. I thought like I was awake, and yet I was unable to move. I tried to move my toes, legs, hands and my fingers. I just couldn't move it at all. Panicking, I started to shout for my mother, father and even my grandfather, but I couldn't hear my own voice.

Sweat poured out of my body. My chest started to feel heavier and heavier. My neck became stiff. I knew that I was awake now, but I couldn't open my eyes that easily.

I tried and tried, and when finally they opened the first thing I saw was a very scary and awful sight of a figure, a black-faced woman sitting right on top of my chest staring at me. In the dimly lit room I could see its reddish burning eyes looking directly at me. I was scared to death. I know I was trying to shout for help at the top of my voice, and yet no sound came out, and it wouldn't let me go as yet.

I could feel the cold sweat running down from my head and feeling very tired as it was hard to breath. Only then I remebered ALLAH (GOD) and recited some prayers my grandfather had taught me. Within seconds the figure disappeared. I stayed awake until morning, fearing the same thing might happen again.

The day following the incident, I always caught the glimpse of a figure from the corner of my eyes. It was the figure of a lady in white facing the wall. I could only glimpse at her back and at her long unkempt curly hair. She was always standing at the same spot, which was at the corner of my room, and it would disappear as fast as it appeared. It was not spooky at all, but very disturbing.

I kept the incident to myself, as I didn't feel like sharing it with my other siblings, beside, I didn't want to frighten them. But the real reason was I was afraid to be embarrassed when they branded me as a coward.

The following nights, I was frightened to go to sleep. Tiredness gave way and I fell asleep automatically. It wasn't surprising when the same frightening incident happened again. After three consecutive s night I couldn't take it anymore. I told my grandfather about it. I also told him about the sighting of shadowy figure in my bedroom.

He reminded me not to forget to say some prayers before going to bed every night. My grandfather told me it was just a passing by spirit, and not to worry too much about it. No spirit, ghost, wild animal, human being or any other living thing could harm us if we remember ALLAH and always ask for HIS protection, he assured me.

True enough, there has been no more sighting or disturbance ever since. From that day onwards I never forgot his advice, just like I couldn't forget the scary experience.

THE GUARD HOUSE

Let's continue with a very interesting recent encounter by a friend of mine, a security guard. This incident happened in January 2013. Whether this story is a real experience or a fiction, it's just a story, and up to you to judge. I prefer if you believe the later. It's not my intention to frighten those people who would normally have to work alone at night like my friend the security guard.

On the day that this incident happened my friend Man was on guard duty at a bungalow house in Bukit Timah Estate, Singapore to replace his colleague who was on medical leave for two days. Man reported for duty at seven o'clock in the evening and was supposed to go off at 7 am the next morning. When he arrived, the morning shift security guard on duty gave him a briefing on what he was supposed to do. He learned that there was a middle aged lady staying all by herself in the big bungalow. She was very kind and never bothered the security guard as long as we're performing our duty. However, she was not at home right at that moment.

His duty was just to make sure of the safety of the lady. He was also supposed to look after the compound to ensure there were no intruders or unauthorized trespassers. There was a comfortable guard house near the gate. This is where he woud be stationed while on duty, the whole night. It was lucky that he didn't have to do clocking. Wow! This guard house was so special. It had a TV set. Normally, on guard duty, we were not supposed to watch TV.

After the earlier guard left, Man went around the compound of the big house once again, just to get himself more familiar with the place. It was extremely quiet. Such a quietness would definitely make one feel eerie, and he started to think those unseen forces. Nevertheless, the thought that the Causcasian lady dared to stay there alone made him brave. He returned to the guard house and sat on the chair and watched TV.

At about, nine o'clock the lady came home in her Volvo. He quickly switched off the TV and opened the gate to let her in. She stopped right in front of him and lowered the side windows. Man quickly greeted her.

'Good evening, Mem.'

'Good evening. Where's Ally?' she asked kindly?

'Ally is sick Mem, and my name is Man.'

Ally was also Man's best friend. He's the regular guard who have been performing the night shift there permanently for the last four years at this bungalow.

'Oh! Dear! Good night,' and she drove on to park her Volvo.

While Man was closing and locking the gate, something made him look at the darkness across of the road. He swore he saw a figure moving in the dark. Perhaps it was a person, as he didn't know exactly what was going on on the ground in front of him. After observing for a full minute, while nothing was happening, Man turned to go back to his guard house. He saw the lights at the first floor of the bungalow were on. Mem was getting ready to go to bed maybe.

Actually, Man felt much relieved, as at least there was another living soul in the house. Man was very hungary. Earlier, he hadn't been in the mood to eat as he was anxiously waiting for Mem to come back. He didn't wish to be caught eating while Mem was back. He had bought a packet of rice with vegetables and fish curry earlier from a food stall when he was on the way to work.

After eating to his heart's content, he sat back, relaxed and watched the TV. Man had given up smoking a year ago for the sake of his family. He had two children now. Otherwise this would be the best time to puff a cigarette. At about midnight all the lights were automatically switched off except for some security lights around the house. He looked around at the now even more eerie compound, the house itself which was an old colonial bngalow looked like a haunted house, and he wondered why this Caucasian lady wanted to stay here alone.

His bladder was full, and he needed to urinate. He went to the back of the house in the dim security light to find the toilet. The back door of the house was locked. He believed the toilet must be in the house kitchen area. The earlier security guard didn't tell him where to find the key. He wouldn't dare to disturb the Mem, who must have been sleeping by now. Neither did he feel like to calling his friend in the wee hour of the morning just to ask about the key.

Where am I supposed to pee then? Man grumbled. He looked around and decided to pee under a tree near the fence. As he was walking hurriedly towards the tree, he heard a hissing sound, 'Shhhhhh', and at the same time he could smell a very sweet scent. Though he tried to ignore it, his goose bump was rising. He proceeded to the tree. He heard the teasing sound again. He quickly did his business and walked back to the guard house to get some water from his mineral water bottle. He would normally cleanse his private parts and his hand after such business.

He didn't feel comfortable. He felt as if something was watching him and now following him from behind. He turned around every few steps, but he didn't see anything. His goose bumps continued standing. He knew something was not right and walked faster. On reaching the guard house, he took the mineral water bottle and washed his hand only. He was just too afraid to be outside of the guard house.

He sat at the desk and tried to sleep, when he heard the 'Shhhhh' sound a few more times followed by the same sweet scent of the frangipain flowers. He ignored this completely. Then there was a knocked at the glass windows at the side of the guard house. Automatically, he looked at the window. From the clear glasses window, he could see a beautiful lady looking at him smilingly. He stared at the beauty. She smiled at him more lovingly.

Such a sweet smile made him felt even more uncomfortable. He knew very well that the gate was locked. How does this lady come in? She looked exactly like Mem. Why should Mem knocked on the window? She could always have come in from the door which was opened at that time if she needed any help from him. He believed what he was facing now was not human.

He turned away his face and ignored her. He was trying hard to put himself to sleep. She knocked at the window again. He looked at the window, and the lady was still standing and smiling even more beautifully. He stared at her, and she kept on smiling invitingly. He turned away his face trying to fight his fear and avoid being hypnotised.

For the third time, there was a knock on the window. This time he turned around but avoid looking at her directly. Instead, he looked at the window frame, wall and the ceiling. He noticed actually there was a curtain there. He quickly reached to draw the curtain and said in a trembling voice, 'I do not disturb you; don't disturb me. Go away!' Ahh! Finally, he thought he had solved the problem. He quickly closed the guard house door. He thought to be safer.

He'd got some peace for few seconds only, as there was a knock on the door now. He ignored it, but the knock was getting louder. He was not sure whether to open the door or not. What if it's Mem? Finally, he got up and open the door. There was no one out side.

He got into the guard room, closed the door; and before he could take a seat there was another knock on the door. He became angry and quickly opened the door as he was afraid that the loud noise might disturb Mem upstairs. But there was nobody there. He went out though he felt very scared.

He went to check the right side of the guard house and then the left side. There was no more sweet scent. It had turned into a foul smell. The smell was so terrible. He braved himself and went to the back of the guard house.

There he met eyes to eyes with three frightening looking figure staring at him angrily with their burning red eyes. He shouted and screamed and tried to run. However, he found himself running on the spot while the being looked at him. Unable to withstand the fright, he felt to the ground and fainted.

Quarter to seven in the morning his replacement came. He called

Man's name, but there was no answer. He phoned the guard house. He could hear the ringing tone himself, but still no answer from Man. He thought that Man must be still fast asleep. He used the padlock to knock it against the gate and at the same time calling Man's name few times. Mem was awakened by the noise. She opened her bedroom window and looked down to see what was the noise was all about.

She gave the signal to the Raju the security guard at the gate to wait, and she came down, still in her pyjamas. As she was nearing the guard house, she saw that Man was lying down on the ground at the back of the guard house. She couldn't wake him up when she had shaken his body a few times.

'What happened to this man? Why didn't he sleep in the guard house?' Mem was wondering. Then she went to the guard house and looked for the key and found it.

'Morning, Mem.' Raju the permanent morning shift guard greeted her as she approached the gate to open it.

'Go and take a look at your friend there,' Mem gave the instruction.

They both went and tried to wake him up.

'I think he has fainted,' said Raju as he felt Man's forehead which was burning hot, 'I'll call the ambulance now, he has a high fever.'

Mem waited with him anxiously. She looked a bit worried. The ambulance arrived a few minutes later and took Man who was still unconscious, to a hospital.

Ally who came to know about the incident, paid a visit to Man who was warded because of his high fever.

He asked Man 'What happened?'

Man told him what he had experienced previous night. Ally asked him whether he had made amy mistake.

Man kept quiet for a while, and then he asked,

'Any way why the back door was locked?' he asked.

'Oh! Ya, Raju didn't tell you that the key for the kitchen door was in the drawer.'

'So where did you eased yourself,' asked Ally again.

'Under the tree near the fence . . . Behind,' he answered shyly.

'No wonder!' Ally said a little louder, 'I think you better find somebody to check on you. I meant a faith healer.'

Man was discharged the next day. He found a faith healer as Ally had suggested. According to the faith healer, Man had trespassed in a place and done something bad there. Nevertheless, a female ghost which saw what he had done had fallen in love with him.

She loved dirty people like him who never wash up after doing their business. It loved the stench of urine. When Man rejected her advances, she told her family to help her to take revenge.

Man admitted what he did willingly.

'You're lucky they only showed themselves up just to frightened you. If they were to possess you, you'd be in bigger trouble.' The faith healer explained.

With the help of the faith healer man was fine again almost immediately. He learnt never ever to pass urine outside the toilet, and that he cleaned up after that.

ONE NIGHT AT THE GRAVES

Would you dare to spend a night in a cemetery? Alone! No! Thank you, I wouldn't dare. However, this desire to spend a night with the dead was just too great to resist. Perhaps it was my grandfather's influenced. He even told me that when he was about fourteen years old, he experienced staying at the graveyard area after midnight. It was a challenge set down by his elder brother who was three years older than him.

So, one night, they sneaked out of their home at around eleven O'clock. Another two friends joined them. It took them about thirty minutes to cycle in the quiet night to the cemetery at Siglap, Singapore. When they had entered the unlocked cemetery gate, they were too afraid to go any further. It was pitch dark with many big trees. Near the gate, at least the street light gave them a little illumination. They convinced themselves to stay put at the stone bench near the gate area rather than go back home. They had come all the way at midnight with one purpose only: to see to the experience.

There, they swore not to scream or utter a word, no matter what they saw or heard as this would only trigger panic in the rest that had yet to experience anything. Whoever experienced something spooky or was too afraid, he could leave the place quietly. He then should wait under the street light about ten meters away from the gate.

The gate area was not lit up. The four of them sat quietly on the long stone bench with a back rest made of stone also. They sat side by side in the darkness of the quiet night. All their eyes were roaming the surroundings, and anxiously looking round at the grave area. What a disappointment!

After sometimes, what they had expected didn't appear. What they could see in the dark was nothing except the the graves, tombstone and trees all over the cemetery ground.

They felt dissapointed as as there were no strange noises that dug into their ears except the sound of crickets, and owls. The sound of dried leaves when little creatures ran on it could be heard clearly. Once in a while the sound of the dead branches or twigs falling and hitting the ground drew their attention. Even the sweet scent that was popular known to be the sign of the presence of the ghost/spirits was not around.

They sat quietly, hoping to see or hear something that they could boast about when they got back home in the morning. At times, they were looking at each other in the dark searching for some signal or tell tale sign. Finally, their eyes gave way and one by one they started to fall asleep while leaning back at the stone bench.

According to my grandfather, his brother was the first one to wake up at about three in the morning. His restlessness awoke the rest. (Later he told the rest that there was something that kept on poking the back of his neck. It happened many times until he was awakened. Earlier on he thought one of us was pulling his leg. So he kept himself alert).

Though he still experienced the poking, he was braving himself not to budge. My grandfather was awakened by the noise made by his elder brother followed by one of his friends. Amin, the oldest among them was sleeping soundly.

This is what my grandfather experienced:

A few minutes later he heard a lady who kept calling his name softly. He didn't turn around though he knew that the voice was coming from his back. The voice got nearer and louder, though he was too afraid, he did not dare to move. He knew that if he went out, it would be worse as he would be alone out there; it would also be scarier. So he kept a deaf ear. Now that sweet scent that they were expecting was really lingering around them.

Suddenly, Ahmad got up slowly and signaled to my grandfather to follow him. Wow! He took the chance at the right time. When they reached the lamp post, Ahmad told him that in the beginning, he saw a beautiful lady walking to and fro just a few meters away in front of them. After some time, it turned into a ghostly white figure,continuing to walk up and down, this time with her head turning left and right violently. He saw that the face had turned ugly and that was when he decided to leave.

He asked my grandfather if he saw it. My grandfather told him he hadn't seen it. He only experienced his name being called a few times and he did smell the sweet scent. My grandfather's brother saw them left, but he didn't bother going with them. Perhaps he didn't see or experience why they had gone. He understood that they might have seen or encountered something.

A few minutes later my grandfather's brother came running out of the gate. He told them what he saw. It was exactly the same as what Ahmad had experienced earlier on. They sat on the grass verge for more than an hour until the sun rose, then they went back to the gate to find Amin.

My grandfather recounted:

'Strange! Our heart was thumping very hard as he was not there. He couldn't have gone back. If he were to leave, we surely would had seen him as from where we were sitting, we could see the main gate clearly. The place still very dark. About half an hour later then there was more light from the rising sun. As we could see further now, we saw Amin lying down on top of one of the graves about ten meters away from the gate.

We hurriedly approached him and woke him up. In a daze he asked what was happening and why he was where he was. He told us he was dreaming of being chased by a group of spirits. He ran around and round jumping over and over many graves until he was so exhausted. He didn't see their faces. However, they screamed with laughter, which was what made him run away away for his life. They cycled home safely together.'

Whenever I think of my grandfather, who had passed away years ago, the same desire to spent a night at a cemetery would recur. I've started to ask my brothers and some friends, searching for a brave soul around if they would like to accompany me. I was shocked at the all Nos answered that I received. Not even one Yes!

'No!' Is the most common answers I received.

'You want to get strangled by the ghost!'

'Are you crazy or what, you've got nothing better to do, is it?' My elder brother answered me.

'Argh! Don't look for trouble until trouble finds you,' another brother commented.

'No! Not me!, I don't want to die screaming in a fright,' said a friend.

'You want to die, is it? Die peacefully OK. Don't die with your eyes bulging our of its socket.'

These are the most common answers from many of my friends. None of them is positive or supportive of my idea. All are against it as if the graveyard is a horrible place to be visited at night.

To go there alone at night? It was really unnecessary. It's too scary. This makes me wonder how some of these people (the caretaker) can stay within the compound of the cemetery with their wife and children. Yet, I've never heard of any of them being strangled to death or died a horrific death.

I explained to them that I just wish to have the feeling. The feeling of being in the cemetery ground, that's all.

'That's unnecessary,' they rebuked me.

'Why don't you join the ghost tour?' A friend suggested to me.

I knew that there are some organized ghost tour at night. I don't fancy that as I tried one once and we experienced nothing spooky, as we were there for barely an hour. We enjoyed the late supper more than we enjoyed the tour.

I never give up, I still would like to spend a night at the cemetery area, but definitely not alone. One day, one of my friends called me and asked,

'Have you got today's newspaper, if not go and buy one, there is a story that might interest you,' he said, and I knew he wouldn't tell me, even if I begged him. Wondering what the news was, without hesitation I went to a nearby shop and bought the newspaper. I read and scrutinized the newspaper from page one anxiously to find out what my friend was referring to.

Finally, I've got it. It was an article about this man and his family who do their work at night at the cemetery ground. He is a tombstone contractor. My friend was right. This news was really great news for me. I called to thank him.

After some searching and phone calls, I finally managed to talk to the man in the article. Wak Man was his name. I told him about my desire and asked permission to spend a night at the cemetery together with him.

'What is the purpose?' He asked.

I did not expect such a question from him. I had not prepared an answer. I never even asked myself why I wanted to spend a night at the cemetery besides just wanting to have the feeling of being at the graves at night. I decided to tell the truth instead of finding other excuses.

'I just wish to feel how is it like to be at the cemetery among the graves, in the middle of the night,' I told him.

'Are you sure that's the only thing you want?'

'Yes! Sir. I've no ulterior motif.'

'If that is the case, I don't mind. Nevertheless, I wish to see you in person first.'

Oh! What a satisfying approval! We made arrangements to meet at his house two days later. Wak Man as he preferred to be called, was a very nice man. He was very jovial and talked a lot. He reminded me again that **Cemetery is not a playground for the living.**

Wak Man said that they were some people who went to the cemetery at night to acquire some black magic. Some would pray for luck and ask for the possible lottery numbers, and many more came with very bad intention that only they themselves understood.

Wak Man gave me tips or rather warnings what to expect when in the cemetery at night. What the dos and don'ts were in the cemetery grounds.

'First of all, he said you'll smell all kinds of things, from sweet scent to the horrid one. Whatever it is, don't say anything, recite your praying in the heart continuously.' was his first advice.

'Secondly,' Wak Man said, 'If you notice or got a glimpse of some unfamiliar figure moving around in the dark, animal, bird or human, don't take any notice of them as it may be the street light and shadows playing in your own pupils. Ignore them completely. Again don't utter a word about it.' He continued to spell out the message to me seriously.

'Thirdly, the sound. Probably, you would be able to hear strange voices—ignore them also. Keep it to yourself, and don't utter a word about it, continue with whatever you are doing and remember the prayer in the heart should continue.'

'I've got a job to do on this coming Saturday night. If you would like to join me, you are welcome.' He said invitingly. Such a good offer doesn't come that often. I immediately agreed and made an arrangement to join him.

I reached his home after dinner at about eight on that Saturday night. Before we left for the cemetery, Wak Man suggested I should clear my bowels and empty my bladder as the toilet would be a distance from where there were going to do their work. It would be very inconvenient to have to visit the toilet at night.

We got there at ten and I helped him to unload some of the tools, the sand, and the cement. Then I sat down in one corner doing what I wanted to do, looking around, hoping to see, hear, smell or anything unexpected. Time passed extremely slowly for me.

The sky was very clear and the three quarter moon gave enough light to see the surroundings clearly. At times, I watched Wak Man, his wife and two other men busily but quietly doing their work. One of the men was mixing the cement while the other one was busy carrying some bricks from the lorry parked nearby.

Once in a while Wak Man would come to sit beside me just to keep me company and share some of his experience. For the past two years he had been moonlighting doing this kind of work. Supprisingly, nothing spooky had happened, nothing frightening, enough and worth telling.

He said that once there was a group of men that came in the middle of the night to one of the graves nearby and did some praying there. He believed they were praying for some lucky numbers. Suddenly, all of them ran out hurriedly. He wondered what was happening as he didn't see anything unususal.

Another story was that once he and his workers spotted two men riding a motorcycle and then walked towards a newly dug grave hole, an empty hole. Wak Man watched them closely as they were about fifty meters away from where he was doing his work. One of them got into the hole and after sometime he came out, and both left hurriedly. Wak Man marked the grave, as he felt something bad had been done. The first thing in the morning he and one of his assistants went to that particular grave hole to check.

True enough, after scrutinizing the particular grave hole for some time, they notice something strange in the grave. Something was buried at the side of the hole. His assistant went into the grave. After removing some soil, he pulled out a small doll made of some women's clothes, and brought it out of the hole. The doll had pins stuck into its body, head, hands and legs. There was a photograph of a woman. It was some kind of black magic work. Wak Man said. Bravely, he removed the pins and threw away the little doll.

Another episode that Wak Man would ever ever forget was when he and his gang saw three men get out off the car and go straight to a particular grave. He saw them carrying a hoe, pail and spade. It was quite bright with torch light at the place where they were doing some digging. Though Wak Man knew they were up to no good, but he was not ready to intefere in other people's business. So they forgot about the grave diggers and concerntrate on their own work.

About an hour later they heard people shouting and saw two men running towards the car who quickly drove off. Wak Man quickly got his gang to follow him to investigate what was happening. When they reached there, a man was lying face down motionless inside the grave that they had dug earlier.

Without hesitation Wak Man called for the Police and an ambulance. Within fifteen minutes they arrived. Wak Man got to give a statement to the Policeman.

The man in the grave was bleeding from under his chin and was still unconcious. With Pak Man and his gang's help they brought him to the surface. The staff nurse tried to revive him, and he regained his conciousness for a few seconds only. They quickly brought him to the ambulance and drove off. Wak Man said that, he was still unable to know what those men's motives were to dig a grave at night—a young girl's grave. Neither did he know what had happened to the injured man.

Wak Man stood up and walked away to continue with his supervision work. A while later, the place became extremely quiet. I started to hear some noises, a buzzing sound all around me, and I got goose pimples. I looked around, trying to figure out what was that sound was and from where it originated.

Cold sweat was running down from my forehead, though I hadn't realized it. I managed to focus the crying sound came from under the ground nearby. I could not pin point from which particular grave the sound came from. The sound was very eerie: the long groaning pain of elderly male and female voices mixed up altogether sounds like a pack of wolves' howling. I wouldn't dare tell Wak Man about it as he had already warned me not to say anything if I heard or saw something strange.

The crying was frightening. At times, it was loud, as if it was afar, and eventually it was very soft as vif it was under my feet, begging for my help. I was not scared at all. Instead this was an enlightening experience for me. I sensed that those dead were in great pain beyond my imagination.

Though I couldn't identify which particular graves the crying was coming from, I was undoubtedly sure it was from more than one, perhaps more than ten graves crying continuously and intermittently one after the other. The sound came from a few graves simultaneously—new and old, near and far. The more I focused, the clearer the sound became. I listen to their cries; my tears dropped profuse, though I did not realize it.

Wak Man, who noticed my behavior came and rubbed my shoulder to comfort me, as if he knew what I was going through now. He told me to be patient and surrender to ALLAH the ALMIGHTY. I just nodded my head. He suggested that I recite 'Surah Al—fateha' (one of the verses from the Quran which every Muslim should Know) as a gift to all the dead and the wandering soul. I didn't know how much I recited of the 'Al—fateha' and how long I cried. One thing was for sure, I shed a lot of tears that mornings, and I don't know when I felt asleep.

Thank God it was dawn when Wak Man woke me up. Wak Man and his company was packing to get ready for home. Their job was neatly completed that morning. I helped them to load the renovation debris onto his lorry nearby. They didn't leave behind anything; not a single litter was left behind.

I was very thankful to Wak Man; there were no words to describe my feeling except a few more tears. How about another night with the dead in the near future? I asked myself. Why not?

Nevertheless, the experience I just had was enough to last a life time. Would I dare to go there alone next time? Yes! No problem—after knowing what was there already, it was unnecessary! I think I`ll leave them alone. Let them rest in peace—RIP—One day sooner or later I`ll have my chance to be there with them forever.

 POSSESSED

My dear cousin is a beautiful seven-years-old girl. She's bright and hardworking. We called her Susi. She was attending an afternoon session primary school. Most of the time in the morning, she would be alone at home as her older brothers and sisters were all gone to school in the morning session.

Susi's father had of course gone to work. Her mother was the only one at home and she had to do a lot of household chores and was always busy in the kitchen. I fondly called them Papa and Mama as they are very close and dear to me.

Susi had no friends and was very lonely everyday. She was always playing on her own. She liked to play with her favorite soft doll. 'Pipi', she called it. She would talk to Pipi all the morning. When her

Mama started to notice this, she tried to stop her. Even so, she would then still continue by whispering discretely.

Mama caught her few times and hid Pipi away. The next morning Susi cried when she couldn't find her. She was big enough and knows that Pipi could not have disappeared just like that. Someone must have taken it.

She cried while searching everywhere in the house for a few days and finally gave up when she couldn't find her any more. A few days later her mother noticed that she had started her dialogue again. Full of curiosity, she went and checked on her in the bedroom. She was there alone. Pipi the doll wasn't there.

It puzzled her, and she decided to make a few further checks. She heard that her daughter was definitely having a conversation with something unseen unsee, but whenever she went closer, she would stop talking.

Mama asked her nervously, 'Who is that Susi?'

'My friend,' she answered.

'Where is she now?' Mama asked curiously.

'There she is over here,' she answered firmly.

'Why can't I see her?' Mama wondered and ignoring the strange feeling.

'She only wants to be my friend.'

'Tell her Mama doesn't like it. Mama doesn't want her to come and talk to you like this,' Mama instructed firmly.

'But Mama! She likes me very much and wants to be my best friend.'

'Mama doesn't like it. Ask him to go away, understand!'

'I have no other friend Mama, please, please,' Susi pleaded.

'You have to stop this nonsense! OK?' Mama became very angry. 'I'll tell Papa about it.'

That night when Papa was getting ready to go to bed Mama told him about the one-sided conversations. Papa didn't take it seriously.

'Children always have their own imaginary friend. This is quite normal laa Mama,' he told Mama.

'Papa you were not at home, you don't know how serious it is.' Mama tried to convince Papa.

'OK, this weekend I'll watch her.'

With that kind of answer Mama felt satisfied.

During the weekend Papa made his own discreet observation, as promised. At the end of the day, he told Mama he didn't see anything strange about Susi's behavior.

The troubled is, Mama said, 'She was never being left alone or lonely during the weekend. She was always in the company of her older brothers and sisters, would you believe me, please.'

It's true that they were happy when they played together, giggling and laughing the whole day as they were playing together. Since Papa didn't believe her, Mama had nothing to say, but deep in her heart, she sensed something is not right with her youngest daughter.

One day a neighbor and also her best friend came for a chit chat. Mama would like to tell her neighbor about her problem. Before she could bring up the subject, Mak Mah the neighbor asked her,

'I sensed something is wrong with your youngest daughter, you know that?'

'What do you mean,' asked Mama.

'She had a friend. She used to talk alone right?' Mak Yah asked.

Again, before she could answer anything Mak Yah told her,

'You better get someone to take a look at her. You just cannot live it alone, do something about it.'

Mak Yah is a woman in her late forties, she had the capabilities to see what is behind the curtain. However, she wouldn't go further. She is not a faith healer. She wouldn't commit herself. She can only give a little advise the rest is up to you to believe it or not, and to get some other people for help. She is a good neighbor and friend.

At night Mama reported to Papa again, more seriously. She told her about Mak Yah advised. Papa agreed to get someone to look into the matter. That person is none other than his own father whom we called Papa G.

The next day was happened to be a Sunday. Papa G arrived in the afternoon. The moment he reached the gate my cousin went hysterical. I was there to witness the incident. It was so exciting as this is the first time I'm seeing a person being possessed.

She started to scream at the top of her voice. She asked Mama and Papa not to allowed Papa G to come into the house. She said that this devil is coming to get her and started to be more vulgar with her screaming and scolding.

When Papa G entered the house, she sat down. She stopped screaming but 'Grrrr' like a lion, and her eyes turning left and right violently. She refused to look at Papa G straight into the eyes.

'Go away go away! Grrrrr grrrrr.' she kept repeating the words and with many more vulgarities.

Calmly, Papa G sat down beside her and asked,

'Why do you come here?'

'Go away, don't disturb me.' she said.

She kept on screaming and refused to answer. At times her eyes would roll up, and we could only see the white eyes. It's was very disgusting. Papa G repeated the question few more times.

Papa G ordered some black pepper. Mama is panting as she doesn't keep any black pepper at home. She asked her elders son to ask from a neighbor. He went and came back in a dash with a bottle of black pepper powder.

'Sorry! I want black pepper seeds, just a few of them will do.' Papa G ordered.

He rushed out again to th neighbor house again to get the pepper seed. For the time being, my dear cousin felt uneasy and still refused to have any direct eye contact with anybody. Her breathing is heavy. Her eyes are rolling wildly to the right and left then up and down. Sometime, I could only see her white eyeballs. It's really frightening, thrilling, but it's a kind of fun to watch at her.

When the black pepper seeds finally arrived he took a few of them and tied it with a white ribbon on her toes, On the left big toe. The black pepper seed was on the toe nails. When ever Papa G put a little preasure on it, she will scream in pain.

'Pain! Pain! Pain!,' she would groaned pitifully.

'Why did you entered her body,' Papa G asked.

There was no answerd. Papa G put a little preasure on her let toe again.

'Don't disturb me. I like her, I like her, Grrrr,' she answered in a very rough voice.

'I want you to get out of her body. You're causing her to be in pain now,' the dialogue continued.

'I don't want, I like her,' She kept on saying it.

Papa G pressed the black pepper seed again and asked her to leave. He recite some verses from the Holy Al Quran and repeated this request few more times. Though she continuously screamed in pain, but the answer is still no. Mama shed tears to see her beloved daughter in pain like that. Papa ensure her that it was not her who was in pain but the spirit.

Finally Papa G stopped the treatment and said he needs to go back home for a while. He left immediately after telling Mama not to let anyone touch or go near her. Papa G stayed nearby, about few minutes walk only from Mama's house.

Everything is so quiet, extreme silence. Everybody were sitting a distant away from her quietly doing nothing; just looking at her beautiful but pitiful face. Half an hour later, Mama asked all of us to go to the kitchen for lunch. Susi was left alone there as she was so tired and had fallen asleep.

After lunch, we all went back to see her who was still sleeping. As I passed by her (I was about fifteen years old at that time), I bend down a bit and pressed her left toe lightly. She screamed on top of her voice and gave everybody a fright. I was shocked and frightened too. At that very moment Papa G also arrived.

Everybody felt relieved. Well, they thought maybe she screamed as Papa G already arrived, not because I pressed her toes. She was now in an hysterical condition, struggling and kicking away more violently as if she wanted to run away from the house. Papa G asked a few male relatives to hold her down while he recited some prayers.

Suddenly, she stared at me.

'Ask him to get out, ask him to get out!' She screamed and pointing all her ten fingers towards me. Everybody looked at me and many sgnaled to me to go out. I left the living room and went out to sit at the veranda shamefully. I missed the most interesting part of the treatment. A few minutes later the door and all the windows were shut closed.

After everything was over, I went to see Mama and Papa and asked for an apology. They told me not to feel guilty and related to me what happened after I left.

It seemed that after all the doors and windows were closed, some interesting dialogues continued where it claimed that it was a 'Toyol' (Toyol is a mischievous little ghost. This ghost normally has a master who kept them for stealing money—I'll give you full details about this most dangerous ghost in my next story.)

It had a master who dismissed him and left him to wander around aimlessly. That's why he is looking for someone's body to reside and be his master. Being a little ghost 'Toyol' also like to play with toys and dolls. When it saw Susi was playing alone everyday he joined her with the intention of making her the Master.

After about half an hour, without further compromise Papa G forced it out and instructed it to enter into a bottle which he brought along with him. It screamed the loudest until I also could hear it from the veranda outside. He plugged the bottle with a cork, and tied a yellow ribbon on the bottle neck.

While he was doing this, Susi fainted. A few minutes later she recovered and was very weak. She got up and went to Mama who grabbed her and kissed her. Papa also gave her a rub on the head and a kiss.

After spending a few more minutes saying his prayers, Papa G instructed someone to throw the bottle into the sea immediately. Susi was back to normal and Mama ensured that she would lways keep a watchfull eye on her. Susi started to help Mama with the household chores and even cooking. She was not allowed to play with her doll alone. There has been no disturbance ever since.

STRANGE ENCOUNTER

Two months ago I visited my uncle in a small village in Central Java. It was about two hours drive from Solo. The place where my uncle lives is a farming area. The people here are extremely friendly. When they heard we out of towners had come, they would pay a visit to welcome and chat. They brought with them some fruits from the village. Most of them are mainly rice field farmers.

At night, the atmosphere was extremely quiet, and the pitch-black surrounding made sitting outside in the covered courtyard a very interesting experience, you could feel the peacefulness. It's a bit cold for people who came from the city like me. To them its most refreshing after tilling the soil under the hot sun during the day. This is the time for them to relax and refresh themselves. Some of the men clad only in a 'sarong'—loincloth, and walk around topless. The atmosphere is cool and breezy. There is no sound of cars at all. Only once in a while you may hear the sound of motorcycles.

While we were chatting on the veranda amidst the smell of thick black home-brewed coffee, the land broker, Ahmed, came on his 100 cc motorcycle. From a distance, when they heard the revving noise of the motorcycle, they knew for sure it was him. It`s was already ten o'clock at night. Why did he come so late this time, my uncle was muttering and wondering.

Ahmed had come a few times before, to study the location of the land that my uncle wanted to sell. Since there was no phone line at my uncle`s house, he`d had to ride all the way just to confirm about tomorrow`s appointment.

'Urgent! Urgent! Tomorrow, I`m going to bring some potential buyers,' he said joyfully and wished the rest of us well. He hoped my uncle would be present tomorrow to meet and bring the potential buyer around. My uncle agreed.

After he was introduced to me, Ahmed joined us chatting. Actually, he could not resist the hot fried bananas and the aroma of home brewed black coffee that my auntie was serving us for supper. The aroma was killing him. He was one joyful fellow. He could not hide his feelings.

He didn't realize how time flies. It was almost midnight when he suddenly realized this, and flustered, he wanted to go home.

'I've got to go home. I've got to go home. I've just gotten married you know.' Everybody laughed.

My uncle advised him to turn left when reaching the big junction, about two kilometers from where we were. 'Do not go straight as it would lead you to past a haunted cemetery, avoid that road,' my uncle told him seriously.

'Nobody in this village dares to go through that route after midnight,' chipped in one of the neighbors.

'Yes! It's true. It had happened on many occasions, people were unable to find their way out, taking the longer route is much safer,' my uncle tried to convince him.

'Many have run back to this village for help. While others were found in the morning on top of one of the trees or lying in the road there,' added the neighbor. Ahmed pretended as if he hadn't heard. He said 'Salam' (bye—bye). He started his motorcycle and set off immediately.

'From his reaction, I believed he wouldn't take our advice seriously, this man was definitely going for the shorter route as it would be ten to fifteen minutes faster.' My uncle broke the silence since Ahmed left. He shook his head in disbelief.

We continued our chatting. We didn't feel like sleeping yet. There were so many interesting stories to be shared. We had not met each other for a very long time. The cool breezes of the night were very nice and I personally did not wish to miss it. Very refreshing. About an hour later while we were still chatting, the quiet and tranquilizing night was disturbed by the revving sound of Ahmed's motorcycle.

Not surprising at all, the brave man was back perspiring profusely. 'Sorry! Pak, Sorry! I couldn't find my way out. I've lost my way Pak,' Ahmed apologized with embarrassment and breathless.

'Lol! Why didn't you turn left as we suggested? You didn't believe us, did you?' Uncle chided him.

'No! NO! Not that Pak! I just wanted to be home much earlier, Pak, Sorry Pak, Sorry Pak for not listening to you earlier.' Ahmed tried to explain while sweeping his sweat with a handkerchief. Auntie brought him a glass of plain water for him to cool off.

'Anyway it's rather late now. You might as well stay here for the night,' my uncle offered Ahmed kindly as he sensed trouble if Ahmed were to go home now.

'Thank you, Pak, but I've to go back or else my wife will start to worry and might think the unthinkable, and I'll be in trouble.' Everybody laughed as Ahmad refused the invitation politely.

'Furthermore, I've got an appointment to meet my client early in the morning.'

Uncle did not stop him, nevertheless. He reminded him again to turn left at the junction. After drinking a glass of plain water, Ahmed formally asked permission once again to leave. Uncle reluctantly let him go. He started the motorcycle and moved off confidently.

My uncle who was known to be able to see the invisible told us that he saw a mysterious figure of a big man, sitting as pillion rider, dramatically it had been sitting side ways as pillion when Ahmed arrived earlier. He was dressed in a long sleeved batik shirt and a dark trousers. His leg and face were not clear. The moment Ahmed stopped his motorcycle, the ghost moved upward, still in that sitting position and disappeared, and he knew that Ahmed was in trouble. That's why he cordially invited Ahmned to stay for the night in his house.

When Ahmed reached that same junction, something strange happened—he heard a thudding sound as if something heavy had dropped behind him, on the pillion seat. Naturally, he turned around to check, but he couldn't see anything. Suddenly, he couldn't control his bike. He tried to turn left, but he couldn't turn the handle, instead it proceeded straight on beyond his control. He applied the break, but it wouldn't halt. He was stunned and kept still.

He knew that the motorcycle was moving for sure, but he couldn't do anything. Thank goodness it finally stalled the engine by itself, and he felt relieved. He kept still on his bike too frightened even to lift a finger. He looked around and realized that he was in the middle of the cemetery, in the graveyard area, and was most definitely not on the main road.

When he looked down, he realized that his bike was right in between two graves. He was extremely frightened, confused, and couldn't understand how he got there. He was unable to balance the bike and fell side ways.

The extreme quietness of the night enabled him to hear sounds that he had never heard before. It was the sound of people screaming, from the lowest pitch to the highest pitch intermittently. They were getting louder and louder, as if they were near, and later it sound so soft as if they were further away. At times, he heard babies cry out loud, and sometimes soft. He also heard the dogs howling, the sounds of cats fighting, toad croaking, and it was unbearable to the ear.

His eyes opened wider to look out for the things that nobody wanted to see. He was getting ready to make a quick dash with his motorcycle when he slipped and fell. His head knocked against the tombstone on the grave. He touched his forehead. He knew he was bleeding. He fainted.

He didn't know how long he remain fainted. When he regained consciousness, awakened by some funny noises, he saw some figures in white slowly coming towards him with their arms at the front as if to scratch him. He got up quickly and started to run. He knew he was running, but he didn't seem to get anywhere. He was running on the same spot.

When those figures appeared right in front of his face, he screamed at the top of his voice and fainted a second time. In the morning, a graveyard caretaker found him sleeping faced down on top one of the graves. His motorcycle was lying beside him.

'Hello, Sir! Hello Sir! Hello! Are you OK?' The caretaker shook his shoulder a few times.

'AAA! Agh!' Ahmed woke up confused and looked around. Thankfully it was day break. He felt relieved but still puzzled.

With the help of the caretaker, he got up still in a daze. The caretaker helped him to push the motorcycle until the main road which was about fifty meters away. Fortunately, his motorcycle did not give him any problem. He thanked the caretaker again and again for helping him. He then proceeded to my uncle's house to seek help.

His jacket was torn and tattered, covered with soil, so were his trousers. There were signs of many small scratches on his legs, hands, body and face too. He related the incident he had experienced last night to my uncle.

'Thanks goodness you are safe. That's most important.' My uncle sympathized with him, and attend to all his needs.

'I wondered, if I was mobbed and molested by a group of ghosts last night,' he said jokingly.

We all laughed.

'Now I've some problem how to explain to my wife about these scratches.' Being jovial he could still create a joke at times of stress like this. He knew that he would have probably lost his customer.

'Tell the truth.' Uncle advised him

To the villagers, the incident was not surprising at all. Such an incident had happened many times before. The victims were always foreigners. I mean people from other parts of the village, especially poor souls like Ahmed, who chose not to heed the villager's advice.

As for the people of this village, they were all well informed about the cemetery and would avoid going near it during the night, unless there was a funeral to be attended. Of course, they would go in a big group.

'PONTIANAK'

Let me tell you one of the stories about this famous 'Pontianak' now. Pontianak is a female ghost similar to the vampire. She always wore white cloth to cover her body. Her long hair always covered her face and it was long until it touched the ground.

One night a loving couple was celebrating the girl's birthday. After having a late-night supper they were driving around aimlessly. Finally, the girl suggested exploring the local cemetery ground. The boy agreed and suddenly became so excited.

It was just a twenty minute drive away from where they were now. When they reached the entrance of the cemetery, the girl felt uncomfortable and wanted to change her mind. She asked her boy friend to turn back. However, her boy friend was too excited to turn back. He assured her,

'Nothing to worry about, OK?'

Without hesitation he turned into the pitch-dark graveyard area. This man became very brave and told her again,

'Don't be afraid. Nothing is going to happen to you. Don't worry, believed me,' and he proceeded on.

'Please, go back now, go back now, I'm so scared,' she was begging him. Actually she saw a lady with long hair in white 'Pontianak' right infront of the car the moment they were in the graveyard are. And that figure moving backwards as the car move forward.

He ignored her and continued to drive slowly, surely he did not noticed the Pontianak. They reached a dead end. He purposely switched off the headlights just to get more thrills. The girl really felt scared and couldn't even say a word. She wanted him turn back. However, he insisted on staying on a little while more.

A few minutes later the girl calmed down. When he saw the girl was so quiet and steady, he suggested they got out of the car. Strangely, the girl didn't resist at all. When he said,

'Let's take a little walk over to the grave area,' she followed him willingly. He held her ice cold hand while she followed him walking slowly on the uneven gravel path in between the graves.

Suddenly, she grabbed his hand tightly.

'Why are you holding my hand? Let me go!' she asked in a very coarse voice.

He got a shock and let her go instantly. He sensed something was wrong, and just didn't know what to do.

He looked at her and said,

'Dear! what happened. Come let's go back; don't frighten me!'

'This is my place, why do you come here?' the coarse voice replied.

He tried to hold her hand. She pushed him away and angrily said, 'Go away.'

Undeterred, he tried to carry her away, strangely she was too heavy. She was not that heavy as he used to carry her before. She didn't budge an inch. She pushed him hard, and he fell on top of one of the graves.

He was too frightened and trembling as he had no idea what to do now. The surrounding area was very dark, and there were no signs of any people around the area. Who would want to come to the graveyard at night?

She moved towards him slowly with a strange sound while both her hands were shoulder level as if wanted to strangle him. Sensing that he was in danger, he got up quickly and ran to the car. She continued to walk towards his car. Without delay, he started the engine and left the place hurriedly.

When he reached the main road, he parked his car at the side, right under a lamp post to calm down. He reached for his mobile phone. Unfortunately, he couldn't get the signal, though the battery was still full. He had no other choice but to get out from the car looking around and hoping for passers by like a taxi driver or motorcyclist for help.

The road was so quiet. After some ten minutes, there was no sign of anybody that he could have asked for help. Suddenly, he heard crying and howling sounds from behind. He saw her running towards him, and thought she was still chasing after him. He got into the car and sped off.

Actually, when she regained consciousness, she found herself sitting on one of the tombstones. She could not remember how she got into the grave yard. The last thing she knew was that when she was still in the car, she felt a little pain in her head. She also felt some dizziness, after which she couldn't remember anything.

Now! When she realized that she was in the middle of the graves, she was very frigthened. She cried and cried, calling for her boy friend, but there was no answer. He was not around. The car was not there either. While crying out aloud, slowly in the dark, she find her way out to the main road. She was so puzzled that he drove off and just left her like that when she had approached him. She sat down, leaning on the lamp post and cried until she fell asleep.

She was fortunate that there was a Police car patrolling the area a few minutes later. They found he sitting motionless on the pavement. The police officer called for an ambulance to send her to the hospital.

It was already day break when she regained consciousness. She was so lethargic and weak. Patiently, the hospital staff finally managed to get her full particulars and help her to call her parent. They came immediately. She related the whole story in a very weak voice to them. Her father called her boy friend to come and explain what was going on. He wouldn't dare to come and see her.

The parents were in a dilemma as who to blame. It had been their daughter who had initiated the idea of exploring the cemetery area. Should she continue her friendship after the boy had performed a very heroic act during the incident?

The young lad came in the afternoon to apologise to her and her family. And took full responsibility for whatever had happened. She was treated for shock and recovered fully and was discharged the next day. She had difficulty in deciding whether to forgive him and continue their relationship or to break it off. She could forgive but she could not forget the gentlemanly act he had performed.

'SI POCHONG'

In Muslim culture when a person is dead, the shroud or the burial garment in which the body is wrapped different from any other culture in this world. We use the moderate materials as the shroud, normally a white cloth. They don't spend or elaborate too much with a complete dress. Three pieces of white fabric—normally cotton fabric is used to wrap around the body after it is has been bathed, cleaned, and dried. A layer of the cotton piece is also used to wrap the body. The three piece of fabric are then used to shroud it from head to toe in three layers. Only the face is exposed.

There is no coffin for the dead. They would then tie it with a strap of white cloth at the end of the legs, the knees, hip, shoulders, and on top of the head. You remember those sweets in a wrapper—it looks exactly the same.

Imagine seeing this white shroud at night in a standing position, in a dark place with a rotten face, eyes dropiping onto the cheek, decayed skin, depending how long he had been dead. The longer they have been dead the worse the face would be.

The body would be placed directly into the hole in the ground. It would then be covered with planks of wood before the soil is put back to cover the hole. They would make the top part which is above the ground slightly higher—like a small hill. Two small tombstones were then buried on the little hill as a marker; one is directly on the head part and one on the leg part.

Now! Imagine seeing the white shroud in the standing position right inside your own house, hiding behind the curtain, at a corner of a room or lying down on/under the bed.

The sighting of 'Si Pochong' is quite common here. Nevertheless, they normally hop all the way back to the house they last lived in. Though they hop about the shroud never touches the ground. They are known to have flown also. If you encounter it when they are on their way home, you can choose to run as fast as you can, or you can just stand there screaming until you urine in you pants. If you're lucky you'll faint and wake up in the morning.

Si Pochong would give you the sign of its presence by some noises and the very stench; imagine a decomposed body, and you cannot trace where the smell came from, or you cannot imagine what the smell would be like.

It is believed that Si Pochong is the soul of a dead person trapped in their shroud. According to some believers, when the bonds are not released, after a few days the body is said to jump out of the grave to return home to alert people, especially the close family members that the soul needs the bonds under its feet to be removed. As its legs are tied Pochong couldn't walk, so on their way they unfortunately scare those crossing its path until the bonds are removed.

When the ties are released, the soul will leave and never to show up anymore. Actually, during the burial, when the body is in the graveyard hole, they would remove it. Sometimes, somehow in some cases they forgot to remove it. Anyway this is only the story. The real reason; it's just another cunning way in which the ghost or the spirits try to misguide the human being into believing in them, to get help from them, and to earn their worship.

There is another belief that Si Pochong also has a master. The master or the practioner of the black magic used it to frighten off his enemy or to make their family life chaotic. The master does this by sending this devil to the particular house against which he may have grudges. The family in that house will experience many strange things happening. For example they may experience a stench at a certain time of the night. They might also find sand in the house every morning when they get up, and in the evening when they came back from work.

No matter how you clean it, the next day the soil/sand will piled up again. The best way to get rid of them is to enhance your praying in the house. With patience and consistency, in the end Si Pochong give up and wouldn`t dare to come into your home as it would feel searing heat and pain if it did.

Another thing which is not the right thing to do is to engage another black magic practitioner to settle this problem. This is where your faith to ALLAH (God) is tested. Besides, the black magic practitioner might compromise with Si Pochong to leave now, but they might come back later to create more havoc.

Si Pochong is also known to show itself only if the house is quiet and only one family member is alone at home. When this person sees the Si Pochong, guess what will happen? This experience is enough to make a person sick or get hysteria and cause a lot of problems to that family, including financial problems. I`ve heard a story about a family whose father was a black magic practitioner.

Si Pochong was one of those spirits that he kept to assist him in his profession as a faith healer. He was known as Bomoh in this region.

Many people come to visit him when he was alive. They came to ask for advice on health problem, financial problems and even love problems. With the help of those spirits, the father helped them to solve their problems successfully. He was well known.

When he knew that his time was about to end, he released many of the spirits. Sometimes he placed them in a bottle, covered them and threw them into the sea. Some of the spirits he managed to return to his gurus as they were still alive. Except one—Si Pochong—where his agreement with it was that he must find another master for it. He tried to pass it down to some friends, but none wanted to associate with a spirit.

He asked his first son, 'Johan, take over my Si Pochong, please.'

Johan was not interested at all. He knew the consequences. Being the eldest and most knowledgeable he warned all his siblings, four of them, not take over anything from their father. His wife had passed away a few years ago under mysterious circumstances. It wasn't surprising when this man called all his children and asked each and every one of them, none wanted to take over. He had no choice.

'You all better be careful because after my death I`ll come back,' the father warned them, 'I`m sorry! It`s too late for me to repent.'

Soon after, the Father became very ill. He didn't want to be admitted to the hospital.

'Let me die at home! Let me die at home,' he asked repeatedly.

Finally father became bed ridden. After three months he started to refuse food and water. They were having a hard time to feed him even a spoon of porridge.

So many strange things started to happen. First of all there would be a foul smell in the father's room at certain days and time. One night, the youngest daughter, Aini alerted the others who were sleeping soundly.

'Brother! Wake up, come, come and look, father is in the kitchen.' Everyone woke up and slowly walked to the kitchen. As they passed their father's bedroom, Johan, the elder brother, pushed the door opened. He thought he saw a figure on the bed. To be sure he switched on the light and confirmed: it was his father. He was lying down on the bed sleeping as usual.

'Oh! Come on! You're disturbing my sleep,' Johan said

'I swear, I saw father at the kitchen near the sink.' She insisted.

When they proceeded to the kitchen, they didn't see anybody. She switched on the kitchen light; she was surprised as there was nobody there.

'I swear! I swear! I saw him there!' Aini was trying to defend herself.

'Father, he is bed ridden; he cannot even lift his hand. How can he walk to the kitchen?' The elder brother was raising his voice, 'Ok! Ok! Let's go to sleep.'

One day the elder brother came home late from work. When he got home, it was already past midnight; it was quiet dark in the house as everybody was sleeping. The moment he opened the door, he saw his father crawling towards the kitchen. He quickly closed the door behind him and when he turned around his father was gone. He switched on the hall light and went straight to his father's room, and he was there, sleeping. Now he knew what Aini actually saw the other day. It was not her imagination. He didn't tell anybody, he do not wish to alarm them.

The last week of father's life was the most frightening for all of them. He never slept or ate. He's was left with just skin and bone, like a skeleton only. His eyes were bulging out and was always turning and turning wildly. Maybe he saw things that the others couldn't see, and that thing was threatening him. He was unable to talk. At times he was having difficulty in breathing. Once in a while he would create loud frightening noise when breathing.

On the last day of his life, he was visited by his favourite nephew. Amir came closer to him to greet him. Amir held his hand, father grasped it tightly. He looked at Amir directly. His big eyes were focused at him in a frightening way, and he seemed to say something to Amir—no clear words came out. When there was no response from Amir, he repeated his effort with much difficulty to say something and shook Amir's hand violently. Finally, Amir just nodded his head. That was it. He passed away immediately. His burial was performed without any problem.

However a few days later, at midnight the big brother heard some one knocking at the door while he was watching TV in the living room with Aini. He went to open the door, and nobody was there. Before he could even put his buttock on the cushion again, he heard another knock. He quickly went to open the door again. He was shocked as he saw his father in the white shroud right in front of the door. His face was starting to rot away.

'Who is that, brother?'

The big brother turned and said, 'There's nobody here.' When he turned to face the door, Si Pocong was gone.

This disturbance happened on many occasions, and all the family members were disturbed. Si Pochong appeared to every single member of the family, with his face getting more and more rotten. The big brother gave a call to his friend, a spiritual healer. He advised him to go into his late father's bedroom and check if there was anything strange thing or any suspicious object. Maybe he had some unfinished job or debt that he needs you to clear it for him.

One night after Johan came back from work, he felt the urge to check his father's bedroom. When he opened the bedroom door, he was shocked to see Si Pochong lying on the bed. He dared not enter the bedroom. It seemed the other family members had had the same experience also.

During the weekend when his friend came over, they cleared the room. He found a thick plastic bag and handed it over to his friend.

'It's in here. I can feel it, it's very hot.'

'What is it?'

'Come, come. You witnessed it.' Among other things there were a few rings with so many kinds of stones; red, black and yellow string; and a few testaments wrapped in black cloth. Some papers were written in languages that they didn't know, and few types of small 'Keris' (Malay dagger). Some of the belongings, they buried, and the rest they threw into the sea. Ever since that day there were no more disturbances or sightings in the house.

However, for the time being, Amir was having some problems. It was understood that the moment Amir nodded his head the spirit had been transferred to him without, his realization. Though he had yet to accept it fully, he could feel that there was always something following behind every day and night. He felt like he was being watched twenty four hours.

He always had nightmare at night. He dreamt the same dream every time—being chased by Si Pochong. On the advice of many friends, he went to see a faith healer accompanied by the big brother who felt responsible for his trouble. He has seen a few spiritual healers but to no avail until the elder brother Johan recommended his friend, who finally managed to get rid of this Si Pochong permanently.

'SI TOYOL'

A 'Toyol' is a little devil toddler. They normally have a master. They are well known as invisible thieves. They would steal money and give it to the master. However, sometimes when the master was dead they would become homeless and strayed around looking for a new master, unless someone was willing to take over to become it's master.

My auntie had recently lost her husband, and she was very sad. She had no children. I always paid her a visit to cheer her up. During one of my visits, she told me about her problem. According to her, the little devil became bolder now by showing itself openly.

She stayed alone in her small one-bedroom apartment. She told me that she was being visited by this little creature. At the beginning, it was signaling its present by moving some light object like the curtain, small pillows and table cloths. Later, it started to roll coins towards her whenever auntie was crying alone. Auntie started to find a lot of coins all over the place in the house; on window frames, under her pillow, on the kitchen table and on the cushions. Normally, a gust of wind would flow in from her back, and that was a signal for the start start.

The first she saw it was when she heard the sound of her bead curtain rattling. She was in the kitchen and bothered, she went to take a look. There it was, dangling and playing at the beads curtain like a swing near the bedroom door.

It looked like a little girl of five years old. It`s curly hair was tied with many ribbons of different colors. It was wearing a tattered long dirtied gown, and its face was black, and some parts were patched with skin that`s extra rough. It was clear that the right eye was not leveling with the left one, but both were extra big. It was a pitiful look. Since then, she used to see it more often. She also observed that its skin was rough and wrinkled in grayish green color. It didn`t make any direct eye contact with her. It continued playing as if it didn`t know that my Auntie was watching it. My Auntie was not a chicken hearted type.

She was more concerned about the money she found strewn all over her house now. She was more afraid that it started to bring back bigger notes; five and ten dollars notes. People who lose money would suspect that this may be the doings of this little devil. If that is so, they might set up a trap to catch it, and it may lead them to her home. She didn't like the idea that she was the master of this little devil.

'Why worry about those coins, perhaps you're forgetful now and placed yours coins everywhere?' I tried to pacify her.

'Yes! I'm old, but I'm not senile!' She raised her voice a little.

'I also used to place many coins all over the place when I came back from work,' I tried to calm her down.

'I used a little pouch to keep all my coins. Now! You listen to this again. How do you explain the incident when one day I was sitting on the bedroom floor reading a magazine, suddenly a twenty cents coin rolled towards me right in front of my face?'

'It wasn't your imagination, right!' I asked.

My word only made her more agitated. She went into her bedroom and brought out a container filled with coins and notes she picked. It was quite heavy; her collection of nearly a year. According to her, nearly a hundred dollars was inside it. She always counted it. Amazingly, when I scrutinized some of the coins, I found that many old one cent coins dated as far back as 1947 was in the container. There are also some rare one quarter cents, and some old coins, which are not of local currencies.

I was now convinced that she was not joking. She really needed my help.'I`ll get my friend to take a look at your place this weekend.' I assured her. She felt relieved now and continued to chat about other topics.

Weekend came very fast. I accompanied my friend who had been practicing as a spiritual healer for some time now, and undoubtedly experience. Auntie expected us and had already opened the front door when we reached her house.

My friend Aji started with some recital. He also brought along with him green beans and some toys and placed them near the place where my auntie always sighted it—near the bedroom door under the bead curtain. Aji said 'Toyol' like to play with green beans.

Nearly two hours later we felt a gush of wind. It had arrived, and started to play with the toys and the green peas. What a waste that I couldn`t see it at all. My auntie saw everything. Surely, Aji saw it and started to have a dialogue with it. Since this type of 'Toyol' is a stray one, it`s easy to deal with them. Normally, the deal will be a straight forward one. He made it promise to leave immediately and never to come back to this place again or risk being caught and thrown into the sea. It would leave without any obligation to stray around the world to find another potential master.

In my auntie's case the 'Toyol' left immediately and promised not to come back again.

'Do you want to be its new master?' Aji caught me with a surprise question.

'Husssh! Don't be crazy man. Yoouuu!!!'

'How about your auntie.'

'No need to ask, why do you think I called for you help?'

If the 'Toyol' had a master, it would only enter a house to steal some cash and left. Nevertheless, it could easily have fallen into the trap and would reveal its master's identity when under threat. If we let it go and make him promise not to come back again, he will obey but not for long. When the master needs money it have to come out and become the thief again.

According to Aji, the master knew when his servant was caught. He would not keep still. He will try his best to release it. Surely, he is afraid of the curse.

'Do you want to know more about this being?'

'That would be very interesting.'

'It's sad that you didn't totally hear the dialogue earlier.'

'Tell me more,' I asked impatiently.

'During the dialogue you can tell him that you want to be his new master. Then he will tell you what are the conditions. If you agreed—That's it, its bound.

'What are the conditions?'

'Normally he wants blood. He will tell you that he only needs to suck a drip of you blood during the full moon only. Don't be fooled, once it started, it wants more and more.'

'How does it takes the blood?'

Auntie who was busy at the kitchen was now serving us hot coffee and some fish crackers. She sat down and joined us to listen to the story. I told her the part that she missed when she was busy in the kitchen.

'Every time the moon is full at night, you'll have to sleep with your foot trailing out of the bed. It will sit there, and bite your toe with its razor sharp teeth and suck your blood.' Aji continued his story.

Aji told us that there is something uniqe about the way they're performing their duties. If it went into a house to steal and saw a stack of money, it would not take all the money. It would always leave some behind.

THE GHOST AT FLOOR TEN

We were working hard to finalize the company accounts. Most of the staff had to work overtime almost every day for the last seven days. Most days

We had to work until nine because the air conditioning for the whole building would be automatically off at this time. Our office was in the busy business district in Raffles Place. However, when night fell the city became like a ghost town. You could hardly see people working around except those few like this staff.

Our Boss was very kind. Besides getting the extra income, we would be given reimbursement for our taxi fare to go home after work. Boss always bought dinner for us too.

Tonight was the deadline. This would be the last night we had to work over time. By hook or by crook, we had to finish our job. Five of us were working very hard. Our boss Mr. Simon was also present to ensure that the job was completed in time. He promised a sumptuous supper when the job was completed.

By nine, we were still unable to finish the task. No choice, we had to open up all the windows for some fresh air. A few minutes past midnight, we eventually completed the task and were getting ready to go home when everybody was attracted to someone outside the window. It was a security guard in his usual uniform and a night cap. He knocked on the opened window and said,

'It's late, why don't you all go home?'

'OK! OK! Amy, our senior answered spontaneously, 'Yap! Yap! We are about to leave,' and glanced at him once more.

Immediately, Amy's face turned pale. She started to hurry them to pack faster. She shouted at Norman to close all the windows quickly. She became stressed.

The boss was ready to lock the door, after the last person switched off all the lighst. Amy was the first one out in a dash. What a surprise! Normally she would be the last one to come out from the office. She looked very pale and was perspiring profusely.

Boss noticed that Amy looked pale, and asked her sympathetically, 'Are you OK? Amy.' Amy just kept quiet, as if she hadn't heard that Mr Simon was talking to her.

'Amy, are you alright!' Mr Simon repeated.

'Yeah! Yeah! I'm OK!'

'Why do you look blank?'

'My mind is at home already,' Amy bluffed to cover up her fright.

All the staff were now out of the office. When we were all In the lift, Amy was hastily wiping the sweat with tissue paper, and looking less nervous now.

Norman, who noticed the changes in her, asked, 'Amy are you alright?' She was calmer now, and assured them that she would be fine but requested someone to send her home. She made an apology for not joining them for the late supper. Everybody agreed that the heavy supper treat should be postponed.

The boss and Norman decided to send Amy home while the rest proceeded to have supper on their own. As the boss drove her home, she felt much better. She looked totally alright when they reached her home. She thanked them for their concern and apprciate it a lot. They waited until she entered her house to ensure that she's really safe.

In the morning, work was as usual. Norman the most talkative in the office was the first one to ask, 'Amy! What was happening to you last night?'

'Do you know which floor we are in?' Amy replied with a question.'

'Ah! Come on I've been working here for more than six years now. We are on the tenth floor. Dear Amy?' Norman replied.

'Did you see the Security Guard outside the window last night?' Amy asked him.

'Yap!' Norman answered, 'and what's wrong with that?'

'Didn't you know there was no corridor out there?' Norman got a shock; he walked to the window to double check with his mouth and eyes wide open. Though he had been working there for years he had never noticed such a thing.

All staff knew about it now, including Mr Simon the boss. Some staff went down during lunch to check with the security guards on duty about the incident. They knew about such an incident. The security guard was the one who gave the description of the ghost that they saw last night. He said not to worry about that as it occurred many times already, and it meant no harm. That Security Guard had actually been a permanent night shift officer before he passed away due to old age.

The boss went to see a Taoist priest and was advised to make some offering in his office. He did that the next day. Later on he made an altar so he could the place offerings almost ever day. When asked, he said he prayed for protection and hoped that with the offering his business would flourish.

16
WOMEN FISHING AT NIGHT

'Women fishing? At night? You must be crazy!' I said.

'No! Not fishing for women! Nowadays women have picked up a new hobby—fishing!'

'I don't like the idea. Women have got better things to do at home.'

'Come on! This is good outing for the family, they also need some kind of recreation to relax.'

'No! Not me. You know in the end you'd have to prepare the fishing tackle for them, set the bait and even throw the fishing line for them—they would just sit there holding the rod.'

'We're floating and living in a pigeon hole, a high rise public housing apartment. Freedoms are very limited. Why don't we go out to stay on the ground?'

'Isn't it enough with a bird's eyes view of the ground?'

'Yes! Don't forget, we're living on an island surrounded by the sea, and yet most of the time our legs didn't touch the ground at all.'

'Is it the sun, the sand and the sea you're longing for?'

'You must know how to swim and fish and enjoy the sun instead of keeping to yourself in a pigeon hole the whole day. We don't do that everyday but only once in while during the weekend the weekend. Are you free to join me?'

'You go ahead. I'm not going to expose my woman to the . . . unnecessary.' Actually I wanted to say something about the ghost, but decided not to highlight it.

'What do you mean?'

'Nothing! I'm just afraid that they may get into trouble.'

With that said my friend is certain to enjoy the weekend with his family. I would prefer. We get back to our old gang and group together just like before we got married—like former times long ago, we disn't have to worry about our safety, the women or the children. We don't have to worry about being robbed or 'rape'.

Besides his wife would definitely bring along his teen age son and his little girl of about five years old along. That is what was worrying me. He's about to expose his wife and little ones to danger.

The place he was going to fish was a very shielded place, well-known for being haunted. Many anglers encountered many kinds of disturbances, even though they came in a group, especially those with women and children. We had been to this place before for camping with a group of six friends. It was dark and quite eerie down there.

Nevertheless, it was very convenient. There was a public toilet near the car park at the entrance to this beach. It was a beautifully design and clean. After the caretaker left after ten pm, the toilet became extremely quiet. The caretaker used to switch his radio quite loud all the time.

We were the only living soul there enjoying our barbeque and guitar and sang along loudly around the camp fire at midnight, an old lady walk passed and tell us to keep quiet and go to sleep.

As if we had been hypnotized all of us went into the camp and fell fast asleep. All of us slept like log until day break. In the morning when all woke up we then realized that there were no other campers or houses around the area where we had set our camp. Who was that old lady? Where did she come from? We were puzzled.

There is a pavement along the beach extending about two hundred meters long. On the right side, it's filled with many tall pine trees. Behind the rows of trees are heavy bushes, that are mostly dark and eerie, and then there is the main road. However, we could hardly hear noises when a car passed by.

On Saturday night, Hisham called me at about 8 pm, and said that he had already reach the place if I wanted to change my mind. I wished him good night and come do back with a good catch.

Surprisingly, I saw his car already in the car park very early on the Sunday morning. I'm his neighbor and lived just opposite his block. I wondered why he came back so early. He had told me yesterday that he would also spend the whole morning at the beach. He'd be back probably after lunch. I thought he might have caught some fish, and didn't want it to rot.

At eleven o'clock Hisham called. 'Meet me at the usual coffee shop in fifteen minutes.'

'OK! See you there,' I answered briefly.

He was already there, and as usual, we would greet each other and shook hands, even though we always meet each other, almost everyday.

'Caught any fish?' I started the conversation.

'Nothing! However, something spooky happened last night.'

The coffee shop owner knew what our favorite drinks were and brought them without us having to order them. We were a regular customers.

Hisham told me that when they arrived there, he was so happy, there were more than twenty people already there. Some were fishing, and some were just sitting around. Some had set tents along the grass verge and some under the pine trees. He had just bought a new tent comfortable enough for six persons. Everybody was busy carrying all the necessary things to stay there for the night. He bought additional fishing gear as his wife was also going to fish that night.

The camp was ready. I was about to get ready with my fishing gear when my wife asked me, 'Where is Mimi? Our little girl!'

'I thought she was with you! Go take a look in the camp.'

'She's not there! Imran you see Mimi or not?'

We were panicky and started to search, shouting for her name. I asked the other campers and anglers whether they had seen our little girl or not. They were very concerned and started to join us in the search. Some of them came equipped with a very good torch light. We combed the area while shouting for her name, but to no avail.

A father's instinct I thought made me walk along the dark and long pavement and continue shouting her name. I knew this little girl could not stray more than five meters from us. How could she have strayed so far? Yet I continued the walk. What a relief in the end. If saw her little figure walking about ten meters ahead of me.

She stopped and I heard her cry and faintly hum at the same time, when she noticed that around her was very dark. By then I was already near her. I picked her up and comforted her. I place her on my neck as she always like to be carried that way and walked back hurriedly.

Half way back I heard my wife and son shouting for me. When I almost reached the camp, I heard them shouting that Mimi was found and she was OK! I felt my hand, shoulder and neck; Mimi was not there. I wondered what was going in, but didn't feel scare at all and surely I wouldn't tell anyone about it. As I reached the site I saw Mimi was clinging onto my wife.

I went to grab her and kiss her and then I shouted to all the campers to thank them. My wife wanted to go home, as she felt very uncomfortable and was worried. I told her to bring Mimi to the camp and try to put her to sleep.

My son and I continued fishing. I noticed all the campers and anglers started to move one after another. In the end only me and my family were left there. The atmosphere became extremely quiet.

My son had also noticed that everybody had left. He felt uneasy and said, 'Pa! Lets go back OK? Everybody had gone except our family.'

'Don't worry, we just started fishing; there are some bites.'

About fifteen minutes later my wife came out of the camp. She had left the torch light switched on in the camp. When she reached me she turned and walked back towards the tent to collect a towel to be used as a shawl as she felt very cold outside. When she unzipped the tent she saw her little girl was sound asleep. But she had company.

Though my wife screamed and screamed she went into the tent to grab Mimi and brought her out of the camp. My son and I, Imran abandoned our gear and dashed towards the tent—less than ten metres away.

'Take a look inside, take a look inside, I'm so scared!' My wife was very jumpy near the tent.

When my son and I took a look inside, there was nothing. But she swore that there had been a long-haired lady in white in the tent, sitting crossed leg and shaking its body wildly near Mimi's head earlier. I glanced at Mimi and she was still sleeping soundly in her mother's arm.

I was rubbing my face with both hands as I didn't know what to do when suddenly, out of nowhere came an old lady, She shouted,

'Go back, go back. There are a lot of ghost around here.'

She continued walking and dissappeard in the dark. We all became dumb and started to pack quietly and left the place immediately.

After driving for about five minutes I started to ask everybody if there were alright. All seemed like they'd just woken up from sleeping, but they relieved that we had left such a horrific place.

'What do you think? Who was that lady?' Hisham asked me.

'I don't know. Don't think too much about her! Most importantly, all of you are safe.'

FARM GHOST

This story was told by one of my Indonesian maids who lived in Semarang, Central Java, Indonesia. In her village, she said, there was a man who behaved strangely. Well! He liked to attend to his farm during the night time only. When asked by the villagers, he would say that he preferred the night because it was cooling, and he could work better at night.

Actually, he didn`t like and couldn`t stand the heat from the sun. The intense heat made him easily tired and sleepy. To him, sleeping was the best thing to do during the day.

His farm was about half a mile away from the village. It was on the outskirts of the village. Every night, once the sun was set. He would proceed to his farm to carry out his chores alone. A brave man they, used to nickname him. Behind his back, they would call him the crazy man. His wife opposed it strongly, fearing the wild animals from the jungle behind the farm would howl at him. He couldn't care less.

He had a little hut built for him to take cover when it rained. He toiled in the soil, removed those unwanted tweeds, distributed pesticides and did repair work to his fences if necessary under the dim light of the moon and the stars. They are many stars, big bright stars shining every night.

He had been attending to his farm in this manner for many years peacefully until one night when he had the experience that totally changed his routine. Its all started when one day, someone, a semi-naked man clad only in his 'sarong' (loincloth) came to his farm and helped him without even being asked.

This particular stranger would come on certain days only. Nevertheless he was very appreciative, so he always shared all his food and drinks with his new partner whenever he came to help him. He hardly noticed the face of his newly found friend as he always kept his distance. Anyway, he noticed there was something strange about the way he walked—he daren't comment.

They became good friends and used to sit down and chat after tilling the ground, it never crossed the farmer's mind to ask for the name of this stranger. He addressed his new friend, 'Bapak' though the friend knew his name and addressed him by his given name. Since this stranger knew his name, he presumed that he must be from the same village.

The stranger seemed to be very knowledgable about farming work. He gave the farmer a lot of tips and techniques on how to get the best out of his farm. It's no wonder that the farmer was always produced best harvest in the village.

However, one night under a dimly lit moon, the farmer's routine was about to change. He was bending and almost crawling to remove some weeds quite near to where his partner was working. He noticed that his partner had the legs of a goat, thin and hairy, no toes and of course not wearing any slippers or boots. The more he looked at it, he became convinced and frightened that this wasn't a human being's legs. He became more frightened when he looked closely, it didn't touch the ground at all. Finally, his own legs moved faster than his body. He sped off like lightning leaving his partner wondering.

He ran as fast as he could until he was out of breath. Nevertheless, he reached the edge of his village and squatted down in the middle of the path as he was too tired to go on any further. He needed to breathe. While gasping for air, he saw a group of five villagers, who greeted him. They asked what had happened to him. He told them about what he had just experienced at his farm. They were convinced and showed him their legs and asked,

'Were they like this?' He fainted when he saw all of them had the same goats' legs.

The villagers obviously found the farmer lying down in the middle of the path early in the morning. They woke him up. He woke up in a daze and went home straight away. He told his wife about his encounter, and from that day onward he never wanted to attend to his farm at night anymore.

LOST

Three teenage cyclists on mountain bikes were cycling along the deserted Bartley Road. They stopped near a bus stand to take a rest and have a drink. The time was already one o'clock in the morning. Not a single car passed by on this lonely road. Many knew that a lot off ghost sightings had been reported in this area; many had caused a serious accident with a number of fatalities.

They preferred to cycle at night as it was cool and there was not much traffic. One of them, Said, realized that behind the bus stand was actually the Muslim's cemetery area.

He alerted his friend, 'Do you know what is behind us?'

The leader, Jefri, who was approaching his twentieth birthday the following year took out his street map and confirmed it was indeed the famous Bidadari Cemetery. They'd cycled very far.

'How about cycling in the graveyard area?' Jefri suggested.

Said agreed excitedly, while the other one, Noh was very reluctant. He admitted he was scared. Knowing he was now beside the graveyard area already made his goose pimples rising.

Jefri had been to the place before, to visit his late grandfather's grave—his father had brought him there during the day. He knew that twenty meters down the road, they would find the site entrance of the cemetery. From there he said, they could cycle about four hundreds metres down the hill. Once they reached the asphalt road, they could turn right towards the main entrance and out of the cemetery ground.

Like it or not, Noh had to follow them. Without delay they proceeded. Led by Jefri, followed by Noh and Said, they were following the gravel path carefully. On both sites were any graves, silent and spooky. This path was down the hill all the way. They were experienced riders. This event was no big problem to them though they were cycling in the dark, and depending on their torch lights only.

They reached the junction in no time. Instead of turning right as he said earlier, Jefri decided to turn left. The others had no choice— but to follow him quietly from behind on this asphalt road. Now! They've to cycle up the hill all the way.

When they reached the top, it was the end of the boundary of the cemetery. On the other site there were empty dark fields with some big spoooky trees here and there. They hung around there for a few minutes silently. They didn't find anything strange after being in the cemetery in the wee hours of the morning and for some time now. None of them experienced any smell or heard strange noises. From the top, all they could see were the shapes of the trees and the tombstone. Some of the trees were very tall.

'Let's go back, let's go back!' Jefri said suddenly.

He led them down the hill once again. They reached the same junction as earlier and proceeded straight confidently. They had been cycling for more than half and hour, and they had yet to see the entrance. Jefri sensed something was wrong. The length of this cemetery ground was only a kilometre long. It shouldn't have taken them so much time to reach the entrance.

They stopped for a while to rest and looked around aimlessly in the total darkness around them. They continued again and yet they weren't able to reach the main gate. They stopped again for the third time.

Noh became so pale, and finally cried when he realized that they had lost their way. Jefri and Said pacified him and told him not to worry. They would surely find their way out. They got off the bikes and walled slowly until they were dead tired. They still couldn't find their way out.

They would not give in so easily, and continued to walk along with their bikes until they felt too tired to go on ay further. They sat down on the asphalt and felt asleep.

When the sun's frst rays touched their face, they woke up. They were separated. Each of them woke up in different parts of the cemetery. They shouted each other's names, and finally all met and gathered at the junction. They had an experience that would not be forgotten for the rest of their life.

This story reminds me of the experience of two taxi drivers that lost their way in separate incidents:

The first case is about a taxi driver who picked up a passenger at almost midnight at the town site. The passenger was a Caucasian man in an army uniform. He directed him to go to the Seletar Base Camp.

The man was very quiet. A scan in the rear mirror in the taxi he could see that the man was wearing a British Army uniform that he had never seen before. He wordered which army battalion he was attached to.

However, after taking another glance at the serious faced man in the rear mirror, he decided not to ask anything. The man was not in the mood to talk. He was neither sober nor sleepy. He had a kind of unfriendly look like a grave God-fearing man. All the way no conversation all.

Travelling after midnight was smooth as there was not much traffic at all on the road. Within half an hour, they reached the Military Base entrance. The taxi driver had to surrender his identity card and was given a Temporarary Visitor Pass. After some questioning and checking in his booth, the guardsman on duty allowed him to pass through. There were so many junctions inside, dimly lit by an old-type street lamp. The camp had many landed houses. He was instructed to turn left, left again, right, left, and then stopped in front of a house.

After paying him the fare, the man got out of the taxi. The taxi driver was counting and taking the change to return it to the man, but when he turned around the man was not there. He got out of his taxi to look for the man. He couldn't find him. How could he walk away and disappeared so fast? He didn't want to think of anything silly, he made a three-point turn and drive off.

He's been driving for a few minutes, and yet he had not reached the main entrance. He knew that when he came in, it was just a two to three minutes drive only. He kept on driving and still, couldn't find his way out. He was lost in the camp are going round and round. Half an hour later, a Military Police jeep flashed its light from the back. He got the message and stopped the taxi. He was out of the taxi when the MP approached him.

'What are you doing here, Sir?'

'I've just sent a passenger and on the way out'

'Are you sure?'

'Yes! Sir!'

'Our report showed that you came in at 12.15 am to pick up passengers!'

'No! No! I was dropping off a passenger, a Causcasian Army officer, I . . . . I presumed.'

'There is no Caucasian Army Officer working or staying in this area. How do you explain that?' The MP replied with a teasing smile.

'Maybe the guardsman can explain this.'

'He reported that you came in alone, with no passenger in your taxi.'

The taxi driver was confused and lost for word.

'Your taxi has been stationed here for more than an hour.'

Feeling more confused now.

'Please Sir, can you lead me out of this place?'

'Sure! You follow us from behind.'

The MP allowed him to go as this was not the first time such an incident happened to taxi drivers who came into the camp and got lost. Many civilians drivers were also found to be lost in this area.

At the Guards room, the taxi driver had to produce the Temporary Pass in order to collect back his own identity card.

He asked the Guardsman 'Are you sure that I came in alone just now?'

'Yes Sir! I've checked the passengers seat and your car boot, remember?'

'Mumbling . . . Not sure.'

'When I asked you whether you wanted to pick up passenger inside. You said yes! That's why I let you through.' The taxi driver moved on and wondering who was that Caucasian man. He didn't remember saying he was picking up a passenger inside the camp. He didn't realize that he had been in the camp for more than two hours. There were no words to describe his feeling right then. He checked his pocket for the fares given by the Caucasian man. He just couldn't remember whether the money had been there before or not. Instead of going on to look for passengers, he went home straight to rest on his mind.

Here is another taxi driver that was also caught lost:

Actually, he could drive the taxi until six in the morning. However, when his wife called him at 11.45 pm to remind him to take his dinner. He decided to pick her up and go for a late supper together as he was now quite near to his home.

His wife was right. Today! He skipped dinner again as the passengers' traffic was non stop. After he dropped off a passenger, another one came. This had been going on for hours. He was so tired and needed a break now. He had already covered the taxi rental, the fuel, five dollars for washing the taxi and still had plenty more money as his earnings for the day.

His wife was already waiting for him at the car park of their house. They had been married for more than thirty years. All their three daughters were married and stayed in their own house. He got a total of three grand-children now. They would come to his house during the weekends.

'Where to?'

'How about the twenty-four hours 'Pratacana'?'

Pratacana was a twenty four hours coffee shop selling all kind of Indians food and drinks. They are famous for the 'Prata'—a kind of fried pan cake eaten with curries. Avery popular food after midnight.

'Is it too far or not?' The wife asked, very concerned.

'It's OK. I'll take a short cut.' There was an old road only known to certain people like him a taxi driver. It's a narrow road, two lanes and two ways road. It's about two kilmetre long. The road was not that busy during the day, but at night it would be totally isolated.

They were entering the road; there were no cars in front or at theback. He drove casually about fifty kilometers an hour. His wife noticed that there was a lady walking slowly by the road side. She took pity on her walking alone at night—maybe she was in some kind of emergency. The wife asked him to slow down and stop slightly in front of the lady. She lowered the side window.

As that lady came near the taxi, she asked her, 'Where are you going?'

The lady lowered her head, the taxi driver took a glimpse at her; he was spellbound; she was the most beautiful lady he had ever seen in this world. Even the Bolywood movie stars were nothing compared with her. Before she could answer, his wife cordially invited her to get into the taxi. The taxi driver took a look at the time, its ten minutes past midnight. He never thought of anything spooky. Furthermore, there was no sign as the sweet scent of the frangipani flower or something else.

The talkative wife was busy and happily chatting with the pretty lady. After knowing where she intended to go the taxi driver moved on. More often than not, he would look into the rear mirror, fascinated with her extreme beauty.

He forgot about his wife who was sitting beside him. If his wife were to notice the way he admired the beautiful lady, surely trouble would be in order. But, she was too busy talking. It was more like a one-way conversation. His wife did the talking all the time. He couldn't follow their conversation as he was busy admiring the beautiful lady.

A big lorry came from the front, flashing its head lights. He understood the signal and moved back to his lane. Here! He then realized that he was still at the same place. He stopped the taxi. It was thirty minutes past midnight. This road was only two kilometers. It wouldn't take a long time to reach the end of the road.

Sensing something was wrong, with both hand he held the steering wheel tightly and said out loudly, 'I knew who you are. Please leave my taxi!'

'Darling! What's wrong with you?'

'Live my taxi now, get lost, get lost!'

'You're so rude!' his wife grumbled.

'Leave now! Leave now!'

He heard the taxi door open and shut. His wife was still grumbling at him when he told his wife 'Take a proper look! Look! There is nobody there!'

The wife turned around, and though she couldn't see anybody outside, she was not convinced. Perhaps the road was dark. She still thought her husband was being rude.

'Do you know what is the time now? Why we are still at this same place?' the taxi driver tried to convince her.

The wife looked around once again; this time she was convinced. She urged her husband to move out of the area faster. Perhaps he had not been driving at all; instead he was enthrall by the beauty; while on the other hand his wife had been hypnotized at that time.

TRAPPED

Din remembered at that time he was a depressed young man of twenty-six-old. He was having trouble at his workplace as well as with his peers; always being bullied and unable to fight back. He had a small build body. His height was only five feet four inches. One of his colleagues who took pity on him introduced him to Pak Bomoh (A spiritual healer as well as a black magic practitioner). A strongman, with the look of a fighter. Din was told that he was nearly seventy years old; yet he was so fit and active and having the strength and power of a young man—primed to look like a pugilist. Unbelievable! Even his hair has no sign of white.

He was invited into a room which was only separated from the living room by a heavy black cloth. An incense burner with a glowing charcoal was lit twenty-four hours in that small cubicle. Pak Bomoh placed a bit of the incense, and the smoke filled the congested room with a little rattling sound. Din coughed a few times, but to his friend and Pak Bomoh it was nothing at all as they were used to it.

He knew Din's intention even without him explaining to him. Din was was amazed. This man really has a super natural power, he said in his own heart.

'You're being bullied! Right?' he asked.

Later, Din thought that it might have been his friend who told him of his intention—a little skepticism playing in his mind. He didn't think so. Earlier on when they finished work at five, they went for dinner together. Then, straight away he brought Din to this little house by bus, which took them nearly an hour, to the outside urban area in Jurong.

'In this world it's like, if you're weak they will bully you. If you're rich, they will envy and respect you, and when you're poor, they will ignore or look down on you. If you're strong and brave they will give you more respect. They wouldn't dare touch you. Pak Bomoh gave a little sermon.

'I'll give you this talisman, and you'll have to take good care of it, but there is some condition that you'll have to follow.'

'Please tell me, Pak.' Din asked excitedly.

'At least once a month on a Thursday night you must smoke the talisman. Understand?'

'Yeah! Yeach! I Understand.'

'You have to read this short (xhdgt gdhhdoem mjjdhdhhd iuiwjsdjs) mantra a hundred times while you burn incense. On top of that you must say this mantra everyday whenever you're leaving your house.'

'Yes! Yes! Yes! OK!'

'How much does it cost, Pak?'

He didnt answer. Then Din remembered his friend had already told him earlier, there was no need to ask about the fee as Pak Bomoh was doing it sincerely to help others. Nevertheless, as a token Din gave him ten dollars when they shook hands to leave.

It was a short mantra in a language that Din and his friend didn't recognized. Before reaching the bus stand Din, who had been quietly reciting it was now already fluent in it. He'd got a super power—a supernatural power for a mere ten dollars. That was unbelievably cheap. Nevertheless, he had to wait and see how it worked on him. He was feeling confident, as if a new energy had been charged into his body. He was so eager to see the result

The next day, Din was working as usual when the bully, a five foot nine middle-aged man came as usual to knock on his head a few times. This time, before the knuckle reached his head Din had already given him a solid punch under his chin, a solid upper cut. The bully fainted. He woke up a few minutes later in a daze.

'You're a fighter, huh! You better watch out Aaa! You! OK!' The bully warned him and walked away.

After work that day at five o'clock Din was confronted by a group of five men including the bully by the bus stand near his workplace. They wanted to beat him up. The bully was not satisfied with the earlier incident. Din fought them off bravely until all ran away for their lives. Din had received a few punches also, but he didn't feel any pain.

From then on, news that Din had floored the big bully and his gang spread fast. Everybody praised Din. They now knew that he was not the type to be bullied. He gained something of a reputation and immediate respect.

Everything was fine at his workplace. He was happy, and there were no more disturbances from the big bully. Instead the big bully tried to befriend and wanted him to join his gang, which Din refused. They remained as good friends.

A few months later Din returned to Pak Bomoh and related the story to him. He gave him fifty dollars as an appreciation. He was pleased with the result. From then on Din became more confident about his ability. Somehow, his social life was lacking, and he missed one thing for sure—a girlfriend. Almost all his colleagues and peer had girlfriends. Some even boasted of a few girls, and some were married with a few kids already. However Din, at twenty six, was still a VIRGIN.

Deep inside his heart, he envied them. He had tried his best and was still unable to win any girl's heart. Some friends introduced him to some girls. All seemed ininterested in him. Then he remembered Pak Bomoh. He had not seen him for the last year. *Maybe Pak Bomoh could help,* Din thought.

Pak Bomoh welcomed him when he came to his home one night. Din had to wait as Pak Bomoh was attending to someone inside his room separated with the drawn curtain.

While sitting outside alone he started to observe the ten-by-ten foot living room. There were no cushions, TV, shelves, or tables or chairs. Guests had to sit on the floor, like he did. Everything was scattered on the floor. The messy living room was an eyesore.

The hall seemed to be in a hell of a mess with an unfolded clothes maintained in corner on the floor of the room. The bundle of clothes was here and there and everywhere. Some boxes were piled up on to of one another, almost reaching the ceiling. Din was very concerned with that—it was a fire hazard. If not only because the main door was kept opened all the time, the smell would choke one to death.

He concluded that Pak Bomoh was not that rich at all. Though he was rich with knowledge that most people didn't have at all or weren't interested interested to know—the spirit world that money couldn't buy. The proof of this was that many people came and saw him for advice. Surely, they gave him some token of their appreciation. That was his only source of income, and he survived that way. Din wondered why Pak Bomoh was still living miserably when people would give him fat money if there were successful.

His attention now focused at Pak Bomoh's wife, who was always busy in the kitchen. She looked like a skeleton roving around the kitchen. She was a quiet lady. She was helping Pak Bomoh with making some medicine for the people who came to seek a cure. Once in a while she would approach the black curtain asking Pak Bomoh if he needed anything.

Din took a look at his watch; it was almost nine o'clock. He had been sitting there for an hour with his mind floating through reflectios. He stretched up and adjusted his sitting position. He thought he might eavesdrop on the conversation between Pak Bomoh and his patient, a middle aged lady. It was too late. He knew that the lady was about to leave when she said, 'Thank you Pak, I shall take my leave now.' He should have done it much earlier.

The curtain was drawn, out came a middle-aged lady who gave him a little smile and walked straight into the kitchen to tell Pak Bomoh's wife that she is leaving. They shook hands, and she left. She glanced at Din shyly and walk out of the open door. 'Ahh! Din. Come over.'

'How are you, Pak?' Din greets Pak Bomoh as he took a seat, crossed leg right in front of him.

He didn't answer Din's greeting. Instead he was busy placing more incense on the live charcoal while his lips were moving mumbling something, in languages that Din had never heard before. Din waited patiently.

'Errrgh!' Pak Bomoh made a strange noise. It was a signal that Din could present his request.

'Actually Pak, I wish to . . .'

'Stopped! I knew what you want. I knew what's in your heart.'

Din didn't object as he knew Pak Bomoh could read his mind—everyones' mind. He knew what this man is capable of.

'Please Pak, I'm really interested in it'

'Let me tell you the condition first.'

'Yeah! What is it Pak? I'm ready to hear it!'

'Are you brave enough to stay alone at the graveyard at night or at a certain place in the thin forest nearby?'

'What has it got to do with this Pak?'

'If you wish, I can teach you how to catch a Pontianak (a female ghost),' Pak Bomoh for the first time looking at him straight in the eye to study his reaction. Of course, he was shocked at being caught with such an unusual question, 'Once you have caught it, this Potianak will be your servant for life. She will obey and do anything you want her to do, whether you want to become rich and famous, whether you want to be a Casanova, or whether you want to hurt other people. She will obey you and fulfil all your wishes. Above all he will protect you from any harm and danger,' Pak Bomoh explained to Din in a soft voices, almost whispering. Din listened carefully.

Being a Muslim, Din knew well that what Pak Bomoh was about to introduce to him was against the religion. He knew that he must always seek help or protection only from the ALMIGHTY.

He believed in The ALMIGHTY, but he had always thought that help from HIM took longer time whereas Pak Bomoh had proven himself within days. Din forgot that ALLAH THE ALMIGHTY had given him a lot of things in this life to enjoy the world, but he couldn't see this. He simply refused to see it.

There were so many things in his mind right now. He kept thinking that Pak Bomoh had already shown him a living example through how he became famous overnight. On the other hand, he was also wondering why Pak Bomoh himself was not living a life of luxury. He wouldn't dare ask him at this juncture.

Pak Bomoh let him think for a while more before he made any decision. He sprinkled in more incense on the charcoal which was covered with ashes now. Din was engrossed in at looking how the ashes gave way as the incense was burned producing a little crackling sound and the required smoke.

'What is the danger and the consequences, Pak?' Din asked.

'There is no turning back. Once you captured it, it's yours forever and no turning back.' Pak Bomoh refused to answer his question.

Din braving himself asked, 'Pardon me, yeah, Pak!, if the Pontianak can really can make me rich, then why are you not that rich, Which evidently you are not, pardon me, yeah Pak.

Surprisingly! Pak Bomoh smiled and followed by a little laughter. He was not at all angry. This was the first time Din see this fierce looking man smiling. At least, it put him at eased.

'I admit. I have control over some of those spirits. But, it all depends on what your intention is. For me, I prefer to be a faith healer helping others to get cured. Though I look fierce—I like to help people.'

'Oh! I See. Sorry Pak!'

'I tell you what, you go back home, think carefully whether you want it or not. Come back here in one week's time if you're still interested. I'll let you know more details about the term, conditions, and consequences. Remember! Once you've decided, there's no turning back!'

Before Din left, Pak Bomoh gave him another term 'This is a secret between you and me; don't leak it to anyone else.'

Din was tired of thinking. On one hand luxury, power and respect, on the other, he was going way against the Islamic teaching. Looking at that old couple, they look alright, still living under one roof. Din has yet to know the reality. What it is like having this devil as a servant? What is it that they want in return? What Din didn't know was that the fee was very high.

Finally, Din chose the short cut to everything. He made up his mind. This was the life that he chose. He wanted to enjoy his life while he was still young. He wanted plenty of money. He thought he was not handsome enough for girls to fall for him. He would like to have some girlfriends just like some of his friends did. Furthermore, he did not intend to settle down as yet.

Exactly a week later, Din dropped by at Pak Bomoh place late at night. As usual, Pak Bomoh was in front of the burning charcoal spreading the incense.

'So! You're ready?'

'Yes Pak, I'm ready. What are the conditions?'

Pak Bomoh took a deep look at Din for few seconds thus making him very uncomfortable. 'OK! The other condition is that you shouldn't fall in love and get married. You can play around with as many girls as you wish. But never fall in love.'

This is what Din had planned. He had no intention of settling down. So this condition was not a problem at all. There was a long quiet moment.

'Do you have any other questions?' Pak Bomoh broke the silence.

'No Pak!'

'Let me recall all the conditions. First, you've got to do ascetisicm. Second remember this is our secret. Do not reveal it to anybody, no matter how much they press on you. Thirdly, you shouldn't fall in love and settle down. Remember all these things, and do not break these promises. THERE IS NO TURNING BACK!' Without hesitation Din agreed.

The next day, as arranged, both were already on their way to the Tuas area at the western part of Singapore. There is a little forest known to be haunted. After about ten minutes trekking, Pak Bomoh spotted a good location. It was a tall banana tree.

'Next Thursday night you'll have to come here alone at night and practice self-denial—asceticism. Are you afraid?'

'No!'

'You come and see me first before you proceeded.'

'OK.'

Thursday night came round very fast. Pak Bomoh gave him a small bottle with a cork and a piece of black thread. He was supposed to tie one end of the thread around the tree and the other end to his own Papa toe.

'Don't be afraid, you will hear many strange noises like people laughing, crying humming. Ignore them. You'll also see many beings come around you to distract your attention, ignore them all. They can never harm you, don't worry.'

'Close your eyes if you wish and recite this short mantra (rkqn dhfh mmmj kek) over and over again until you could see a mist in the form of a human figure being suck into the bottle. When you hear the sound like people asking for help coming out from the bottle, cover it and bring it back to me.'

'If you have no question, GO NOW!'

Like being hypnotized Din follow the instruction without feeling any fear. It was a full moon night, he didn't need his torch light to trek across the track he passed few days ago. He reached the destination without any difficulties. He laid down a poncho on the ground under the tree. He took out the thread from his pocket and tie one end around the trunk pf the tree, and the other end at his Papa toe.

He sat right under the heart of the banana tree and started to recite the short mantra given to him by Pak Bomoh over and over. The gentle glow of the moon had mysterious aura that left him spellbound. He was so confident and did not feel at all afraid. Perhaps the greed for luxury made him feel this way.

CAUTION!! Do not try this at home! When you do it without the proper instruction from the expert, you can be possessed and fall seriously ill. You can end up in a Mental Intitution, if people find you, a mad person—a zombie. If this happened, it's not easy to cure as you're the one who made the mistake by intruding into unseen territory. The worst that can happen that you are scratched and strangled to death.

SO! DON'T TRY THIS AT HOME—IT'S NOT WORTH IT. Make no mistake, the thread and the bottle that were given to Din had already been neutralized with mantras by Pak Bomoh. The spirit would be induced to enter the bottle and not the person. The person is protected from being attacked or possessed.

It was a clear sky. The moon is at its fullest at about one in the morning. It was so bright that he can see the shadow of the banana tree, dancing on the ground when blown by the night breeze. So did those trees surround him. Occassionally, the serenity of the night was shattered by the piercing howl of wind. Finally, he reached the alpha level and started to be drifted into the other dimension. He lets it float.

He saw this beauty smiling lovingly once in a while when he opened his eyes. He continued with the mantras. He started to hear all kinds of sound that he never heard before. Though he closed his eyes, he could still sense many kinds of genie lurking around him.

Some were trying to frighten him by jumping at him, but he didn't feel anything, no physical contact at all. May be it was his imagination only. In the end, he was forced to open his eyes and saw a horrible looking spirit in a white robe sitting and shaking its body wildly right in front of him. He was not afraid at all. He closed his eyes and continued to recite his mantra.

A few minutes later he opened his eyes, and the spirit was still there sitting quietly. Then, it turned into a mist and was sucked into the bottle. He watched it anxiously. True enough, he heard the spirit starting to scream for help intermittently with low and hig-pitched voices. As instructed by Pak Bomoh, he covered the bottle properly and packed it up.

He reached Pak Bomoh's house at almost four in the morning.

Surprisingly, he was still awake. The door was still open. Pak Bomoh was waiting for him expectantly in his living room. Perhaps his wife was sleeping behind the thick curtain.

'Good! Good! Good! You've done it.'

He gave the bottle to him. Pak Bomoh sprinkled some incense on the charcoal and placed the bottle on top of it and reciting some mantras.

After ten minutes, he returned it to Din. 'It's all yours now! Remember! There is no turning back.'

Din took his leave and went straight home. He took some urgent leave that day, and spent the whole day sleeping. His lifestyle was about to change. He got a lot of chances to do overtime, and he worked hard and was soon promoted to supervisor. He was much happier and there was a glow on his face. Girls started to be attracted to him. Wherever he went, he turned the girls' heads. Now he was changing girlfriends as often as he was changing his underwear.

In the beginning, his trouble was at home when his sister got married. His brother-in-law was a religious man. Everyday he would perform his Muslim obligation and recite the Al-Quran late into the night. Din felt very hot and uneasy whenever he heard the Al-Quran is recited by his brother-in-law. He also had a lot of frightening nightmares.

Almost every night his Pontianak appeared in his dream as if in pain and asked him to move out of the house. A few months later he moved to a small apartment where he had more privacy.

Here, he lived peacefully for ten years without any disturbances, no trouble or being bullied. He enjoyed life to the full. He was a Casanova as well as a playboy. Money was not a problem to him, until one day.

One day he met a girl at a shop nearby his house. They looked at each other for more than the usual glance. Din's heart was thumping hard. He could hear his own heart beat. The girl smiled and walked way shyly. He had fallen in love at first sight. He started to miss his angel. One day he took a leave just to follow her and find out where she lived. One day he took leave just to follow her to where she worked. One day he couldn't stand it any longer and approached the girl directly. One day after a few dates he told her how much he loved her.

The next day he remembered his promise to Pak Bomoh or with the Pontianak rather. The next day he was at Pak Bomoh house, and disappointed when he found out that the old man was very ill.

'You're too late.'

'Seriously, Pak, I want to give this up.'

'You shouldn't do it, and also I can't help you.' Din was begging Pak Bomoh to help him take back the Pontianak that he had given him a decade ago. He did promise that if he wanted to stop the service of the Pontianak, he could always return it to him.

'Pak! Please help me, I have fallen in love and want to get married.'

'Din, you take a look at me closely. I'm suffering now. I've managed to remove some of those spirits that I have, but many more are still haunting me. I'm facing the consequences right now—only the ALMIGHTY knows how terrible and painful.'

It was a pitiful look. The old man who was once five feet seven inches was now shrunk tremendously and look very skinny and tiny. He looked very much smaller than the man Din met ten years ago. Din almost couldn't recognize him. The wrinkles on his face overlapped each other. The fair skin was now now turned so dark, especially around both eyes. Anyway he was nearly ninety years old.

In fact, his waist had once been 44 inches was now barely 24 inches—the waist of Miss Universe contestants. He was left with skin and bone just like his wife. His eyes were weary with heavy black rings around them. The man he used to seek and ask for advice was now helpless himself.

Two months later he paid another visit hoping to see Pak Bomoh again. Instead he was there to witness Pak Bomoh's last breath. It saddened him so much. However, he was determined to marry the girl whom he loved so much. She was really an angel sent to him. She was an old fashioned virgin. Din never even dared to touch her hand when they went out dating. She was too shy and threatened not to meet him again if he insisted. Din was amused and alway smiled happily. Those girls he met before were the opposite. She was just too naive, maybe that's why Din liked her.

After doing some thinking for a few nights Din decided to marry her although he was about to break the agreement with the spirit. He did not know what was ahead, what was going to happen, he didn't know what the consequences would be. He just couldn't care less.

He repented. He turned a new leaf. He started to rely on the ALMIGHTY. His only hope was than the ALMIGHTY would help him, even though he created havoc in his own life. Din started to attend religious classes and performing and worshipping ALLAH as a Muslim should do. Under the guidance of an Ustaz (Islamic religious teacher), he changed for the better. He observed the Muslim's five pillar strictly.

No doubt that he had many nightmares and sleepless nights. However, he managed to overcome this by reciting the Holy Al-Quran every night. He was glad that nothing strange was happening to him. No retribution had taken place so far and Din thought that it was over.

He was so confident and had no idea how wrong he was. He never knew that the Potianak had its own agenda. It was still lurking around him waiting for the right time to strike and claim what was its right. He forgot that he was owing something and no matter what, he had to pay for it.

Only he himself knew why he had got to pay for it. But with What?

When? And How? The late Pak Bomoh never had a chance to explain to him about this. He knew that the Ustaz might know something about this. His own ego stopped him from asking for help. He was too ashamed to tell other people that he was keeping a Pontianak. He rather continued to keep the secret and try to face what ever the consequences might be for himself.

Din married the virgin and live happily for a year. The trouble started to surface when his wife was three months pregnant. His wife started to feel uneasy and scared whenever Din was not at home, especially at night. She complained to him that she used to see the shadow of a lady walking freely around the house. Din comforted his wife and encouraged her not to be afraid as it could be her own imagination only.

Things got worse when she was five months pregnant. She used to dream that there was this lady who came in her dream and wanted to claim the baby. She would scream and woke up frightened. Din promise that he would stay home during the night. When he was at home reading the Al-Quran, everything was fine. His wife felt more secured.

Until one unfortunate night, Din was called up to work at night as there were some emergencies, two of his colleagues were on medical leave while another one was on leave and out of the country on holiday. His wife was crying when he had to leave for works at seven that night.

Around eleven that night, his wife called his office. She was crying and asked him to come home immediately. She said there was a figure at the kitchen when she wanted to take some water earlier. That figure walked towards her with a 'brrrrr' like a hungry lion. She was so afraid that she ran and stumbled on the dining table, and she had screamed in pain and fear. When she looked back the figure was now crawling slowly towards her.

She got up in a hurry and with much difficulty and walked to the bedroom. She found herself bleeding. At that moment, she heard a knock on the door followed by a scratching sound. Din heard her scream at the top of her voice, then silence. Din shouted, 'Hello! Helllo!' A few times but there was no response. Din told his supervisor and left for home immediately.

When he reached home twenty minutes later, the whole house was lit up. The hall, kitchen and the toilet. He saw some traces of blood on the floor. He quickly went to the bedroom and saw his wife had fainted and there was pool of blood on the bed.

He immediately called for an ambulance. She was brought to the hospital. The doctor reported that she had had a miscarriage but was in a stable condition. She woke up and discovered that her stomach was flattened. She cried and cried as she knew that she had had a miscarriage. She became remorseful and was never the same again.

She got mood swings, always throwing tantrums and at times remained extremely quiet. She liked to sit near the windows and comb her hair, as if she had got very long hair. He knew she was being possessed.

Din approached the Ustaz for help. The Ustaz came immediately. After reciting some verses from Al-Quran, she started to scream in pain. Ustaz pacified Din telling him not to worry. The one who was in pain and screaming was not his wife but the spirit. The dialogue started between the Ustaz and the Pontianak who spoke in a rough and coarse voice.

'Go away don't disturb me, pain Argh . . . . Argh . . .'

'You must leave her body, you ae not supposed to possess her.'

'She's mine, she's mine, leave me alone.'

'Who sent you here?'

'Nobody! I came to claim my right. I've a right over her.'

'Who is your master?'

'Argh . . . Arghh . . . Argh . . .' It refused to reveal this.

'Who is your Master. Come on. Who is your master? Otherwise I'll put you in more pain.'

By reciting some selected verses from Al Quran it would burn the spirit thus, causing it to be in great pain. Unable to withstand the pain, and naturally a traitor the spirit said,

'Aaarg! My Master is Abidin Bin Salim.' The voice was loud and clear.

'Now! You better get out of her body before I cause you more pain.'

'I'll leave for now. OK! I'll come back later for sure . . . Argh . . .'

Ustaz and Din left the bedroom to let his wife who was exhausted rest. Ustaz faced Din at the cushion in the hall and asked him what he had got to say about his name being mentioned as the Master. Din made a complete denial.

'Din, I'm not accusing you. If you tell me the truth it'll be much easier to treat you wife.'

Din just looked down on the floor. He wouldn't dare look Ustaz in the eye.

'I pity your wife, if it's a stray spirit, it's much easier to deal with.

Even if it's under the command of some Masters, I could still make a deal with it; but if it's from you, her own husband, then it's very difficult to treat.'

Ustaz made it clear that he didn't meant to accuse him, but that was what the spirits claimed. If it was Din's, Ustaz wouldn't know what the agreement was like when he took the spirit. It may take months or years before she could recover completely, with ALLAH'S (God) WILL.

However, soon Din's heart couldn't take it. It was between ego vs love—his love for his wife was stronger. He wept. He told Ustaz everything from the beginning until that point.

He went inside the room and took the bottle and showed it to Ustaz. Din agreed to throw it away. Ustaz preferred if Din himself threw it away, normally into the sea. Ustaz reminded Din to be more patient as the treatment would take a very long time.

When Ustaz was about to leave Din's parents-in-law came. They went straight to see their daughter while Din ask permission to go out with Ustaz for a bit. When Din came back, they suggested that Din move in and stay with them. They we're very concerned about their daughter's well being. Din agreed, and he moved in to his parent-in-law house immediately. A week later Ustaz was summoned when his wife was possessed. After the same treatment, the spirit left, swearing that it would come back again to claim its right.

Two weeks later there was nother incident, followed by yet another a month later. The next possession happened six months later. The treatment was the same. They would recite some verses from the Al-Quran, only this time the parents-in-law and few more relative joined in the ritual. The spirit got weaker and weaker over time.

And finally, after three years of consistent treatment, Ustaz declared Din's wife to be fully recovered, as the spirit was unable to come near her any longer. She was now joining the family to recite the Al-Quran everyday.

THE THIRD EYE

A usual, he would take a cab home whenever he worked overtime till late in the night. This was the five-star hotel company policy. He left his office exactly at midnight. He knew if he came out earlier it wasn't easy to get a cab. Those cab drivers would probably take cover; take their break or hide somewhere until midnight so that they could earn the extra fifty percent midnight surcharge.

The moment he stepped out of the hotel lobby, an empty taxi came in. There were other people waiting for the taxi; this was his lucky night. He got into the taxi. He took the back seat as he wanted to relax and probably get a little nap on the way. The journey to his home at Yishun would take about thirty minutes.

He was wrong. The taxi driver was a very talkative man. A middle-agedcabbie man, the cabbie didn't give him a chance to doze off at all. The moment he picked him up he started to talk almost nonstop. He was boasting about his earlier years as a gangster. He could see that the cabbie had some tattoos on his arm, tattoos of a tiger and numbers which he could not see clearly. In the olden days in Singapore, a tattoo was a symbol of gangsterism.

Different designs of tattoos referred to different groups of gangs. There were tigers, lion, eagles and many more. They were controlling various parts of this little island. He just listened and forgot to tell him that he preferred to take the highway all the way. It was too late to say this as the taxi had already turned onto the haunted Mt Pleasant Road, a short-cut. He didn't like to pass along this road, as it was full of ghosts—he could see them.

'You should have taken the highway', he said.

'Why? You scared to go by this road. Ahh!. Don't be afraid la!'

The moment he turned into this dimly lit and lonely road, he spotted a few figures at the side of the road, in the middle of the road and on top of the tree in front. He just kept quiet, trying not to focus to any of these figures. He knew there we're so many of them in this area. This was not the first time he had passed along this road. That's why he was not in favor of going along this road, especially at night.

It's not because he was scared, but the trouble was, some of them might follow him home as he would have followed others who passed at this area. If they realized that he could see them, they would try to attract their attention. He had been told this by some gurus. First of all, they wanted to befriend people like him and later would omake use of him to mislead more and more people. He must always be alert not to start any communication with them.

'Don't Worry, whie I'm around they wouldn't dare to come out.' The taxi driver boasted and laughed.

He shut his mouth. He believed the taxi driver didn't see what he saw. Sometime he closed his eyes just to avoid what he was seeing. Suddenly, there was a thudding sound on the bonnet. He saw and recognized that it was a Pontianak (a female ghost). It was sitting right on the taxi's bonnet and starring hard at the taxi driver. He believed that the taxi driver didn't see it. Nevertheless he seemed to have some difficulties steering the taxi. He closed his for a while. He could feel the taxi swaying. He opened his eyes to see what was happening.

The Pontianak was still there, blocking part of the taxi driver's view. That's why he was having some difficulties driving. It was fortunate that there was no other traffic driving from the opposite direction; if they had bee, probably a head on collission would have been unavoidable.

'Are you OK?'

'Don't worry laaa, I'm just a little tired.'

He took a glance; it still there, and he was surprised it didn't slide off; instead it sat there like a heavy statue. Even its long hair remained intact, downwards. He believd if a person with long hair were to sit there, surely the hair would be blown backwards.

The taxi driver looked nervous; he was sweating and asked permission to smoke. He allowed him and wound down his side window. Finally, they were out of that haunted road. The taxi driver was at ease now. He put out his cigarette and switch on the AC. He noticed that the Pontianak was not there any more. This talkative man became a mute. He didn't say a word and was driving as usual for about fifteen minutes while he was still trying to steal some sleep.

Five minutes before reaching his apartment, the Pontianak reappeared. Again, he didn't think that the taxi driver saw it. But, his reaction became indifferent. He looked so stressed and he could see that the taxi driver was perspiring profusely again. The taxi driver took a handkerchief from the side pocket and wiped his sweat hurriedly.

He reached his destination and asked the taxi driver to stop near his block. He paid him and asked for the receipt. He needed the receipt to apply for a reimbursment later. After he had been dropped off, he glanced at the taxi and saw that the 'Pontianak' was still sitting on the bonnet of the taxi. The taxi driver drove off and stopped about twenty metres away under a street light. He stopped walking to see what was going on or what was about to happen.

He saw the taxi drive come out out of his taxi and light a cigarette, and proceed slowly towards the lamp post. The taxi driver squatted down on the grass verge and continued smoking. Perhaps he was very stressed and was trying to cool himself down. He entered the lobby and couldn't see what happen to the boastful taxi driver.

One evening, a few weeks later he happened to meet the same taxi driver at the hotel where he worked. The taxi driver parked his taxi quickly and chased after him.

'Hello! Hello!' he shouted, oblivious to the many people in the lobby many people the lobby. Everybody looked at them. The cabbie stopped walking and had already reached him and tappped his shoulder.

'Do you remember me?' he asked.

'Yes! I am sure to remember you.' He somehow somehow dragged him to sit in the the hotel lounge.

'That night, were you OK or not when you reached home?'

'Yes! I was OK. What happened?'

'Ai Yeah! After I had smoked two cigarettes, I had continued driving. I saw some people along the road, but they appeared not to notice my taxi at all; some hailed the taxi behind mine.'

'Really!'

'Yeah!' the taxi driver convinced him. 'Actually my taxi smelt very bad. I have to open the window. A few mniutes later I received a call to fetch a Caucasian man at Sembawang Park who needed a taxi to go to Changi Airport. I took the booking; its good money. When the 'Ang Mo' (better known for the Caucasian man) asked me what kind of perfume I used for my taxi. He didn't believe me when I said I didn't use any perfume. He didn't like the smell at all and kept scolding me all the way to the airport. He scolded me for not cleaning the taxi properly and resort to apply a lot of perfume. When we reached there, he refused to pay and just slammed the door and walked away quickly. I didn't have a chance to argue with him at all as when I came out of the taxi to confront him, he'd already disappeared.'

'Friend, next time becareful with what what you say.' He said to the cabbie kindly. 'It's better to keep your mouth shut if you're unable to come up with something good.'

Fortunately, the cabbie could take his advice and ready to leave.

'I know, I know, Thank You Haa!'

He smiled, at least he'd made him happpy after he shared his miserable experience.

OFFENDED

The three of us have been buddies since the school time. Now all of us are married and have our own families to look after. It's obvious that once I got married five years ago, we became a little distant. A year later Lim also got married, followed by Gopal. Our relationships are unique because we are from three different races, cultures and family background. Yet we got along very well.

Lately, after a lapse of five years, we started to meet more often. Our wives relaxed the marriage chain slightly. Now, we met each other more often than we meet our own siblings. Instead of hanging around and doing nothing, we wanted to pick up a new hobby together. We brainstormed a few ideas, and finally chose fishing.

None of us knew about fishing. We had to learn from scratch. We were told that Sembawang Park was one of the best places for fishing from the shore. We went to survey the area one Sunday morning. There were some people we call anglers at the beach under the morning sun, already fishing. We befriended them. They we`re kind enough to explain to us in great details how to fish in this particular area. They suggested night fishing as it was much cooler and yielded a better catch.

The following Saturday night after dinner we proceeded to Sembawang Park again.

'Where do people go here?' Gopal asked impatiently.

'Wait, people fish at the beach there, not here in the park.' I answered.

The park was dimly lit by the park light. But as we walked towards the beach, the place was getting very dark. It was a moonless night. At a distance we could see dark figure in groups of people stannding and moving along the beach.

The three of us walked faster as we`re so eager to find out how was the catch that night? We met the first group of three youngsters and talked to them. They had just arrived and had yet to catch anything. We continued to walk further where another group of anglers were fishing. Oh! no! This was a family outing. While the father was fishing the children and the mother were busy at the camp fire roasting fish, crabs and marshmallows.

'This is a good idea, Man! We could bring our families for camping here,' Lim suggested.

'You are silly Ah! I think there are many ghosts here,' Gopal chided him.

'Aiyo! We'll come in a big family so we would not be disturbed!'

I just kept quiet.

We reached a river bank, and that was the end of the beach. We hung around there for a while, smoking cigerettes and chatting. All of us are casual smokers. As soon as we finished we made a move, as there was nothing much to see in the dark except those buildings' lights across the sea. It's the Johor water front city.

We've been walking for half an hour. I just couldn't imagine that we'd been walking so far. Finally, we saw the car park lights a distance away, and decided to take a short cut through a path with many big pine trees. We were racing. Gopal was way ahead of us as usual. He's a fast runner. I was very close to Lim. He had stepped on something; he stumbled and almost fell on to me.

'What happened?'

'I stepped on something.'

'What is it? Are you injured?'

'I'm OK.'

Using the the light from our mobile phones, we tried to search what it was. What had made Lim fall? It was a paper plate and some small porcelain bowls, normally used by the Chinese for offering. Lim recognized it. He had accidently kicked the whole thing upside-down. There was nothing in the bowl. There were some busicuits and a food waste mark on the paper plate. Perhaps someone had made an offering there, and it must have been there for quiet sometime.

Gopal must have reached the car and wondered why we we're so slow. Lim got up and walked back slowly. Lim was having some difficulties with his breathing though he had no history of asthmatic. After a while he was breathing as normal. We reached the car park, greeted by a big laugh from Gopal, who was waiting for us. He shut up when he realized that Lim's face was pale and started to have difficulty breathing.

All the way home everything was fine. At about, eleven that night. He gave Lim a call. Lim said he was fine.

The next day again Lim was having some difficulties in breathing once in a while. He went to his family doctor who said there was nothing wrong with him. He was given some pills. The doctor wanted him to rest at home. Lim was glad as he was covered with two days' medical leave. The medicine made him drowsy and sleepy. That's what he did the whole day, sleep.

That night after twelve midnight Lim was having the attack again. His short breathing had turned out to be more serious. The wife called an ambulance and sent him to the hospital. He was totally calm when they reached the hospital. After checking on him thoroughly, the doctor found that there was nothing wrong with him at all. He was sent home. They scolded them for wasting hospital time as a thorough check revealed there was nothing.

Gopal and I went to visit Lim in the evening after work. He was not Ok. He behaved like people having an asthma attack. He had difficulties with breathing in. Every intake of air was as difficult as when he breathed out.

Lim told me that he didn't feel good about the Saturday night incident. He sensed that it might have had something to do with it. He happened to know a Taoist Priest staying nearby and asked us to accompany him. He wished to ask him for advice. Lim got ready, and we planned to go there immediately. Gopal was making some excuses. He knew he was actually afraid to go to such places.

I accompanied Lim to the Taoist Priest home. It was just a few minutes drive away. When we reached there, the Taoist Priest, Mr.

Juung was ever ready to receive visitors. He's a very nice man, always smiling, and he had very clear face—serene looking.

Mr. Juung knew what had happened. Suddenly, he sat upright with his two hands holding the side guard of his settee. His face turned red, his eyebrows tilted upwards; he was in contact with the bad spirit. Once in a while we could hear him murmuring in a Mandarin language. I don't know if we can call this a trance, or something else. It lasted for a full ten minutes.

Mr Juung was back to his normal self; he explained what had happened. He asked Lim to confirm that he had kicked a few bowls at the park near Sembawang Beach. The spirit was offended at that moment; it was sitting hoping for someone to make another offering. Instead, he was almost crushed to the ground as Lim was stumbling and kicking it. The spirit wanted him to ask for an apology and compensation.

Is there such a thing? I said in my heart.

'You better believe it.' Mr Juung said loudly and firmly as if he knew what was in my heart.

Lim just sat there. He didn't know what to do. He was a little skeptical. He looked up at me as if asking for some ideas. I avoided eye contact as I didn't wish to influence him. I could not help him as I'm a Muslim, and I wouldn't have agreed to the deal.

'If not! The spirit will hunt you forever—until you die.' Mr Juung continued.

'Wah! So, serious man!' Lim was shocked.

'It's a good thing that he wanted to negotiate and compromise with me.'

'But how?'

'First of all, do you agree to ask for an apology?'

'Yes! I think I have to,' Lim confessed firmly.

'This is what you have to do.' Mr. Juung explained in great details to Lim in Mandarin. Being Chinese himself, he knew what he was supposed to prepare and do.

On the way to a market nearby, Lim explained to me that he had to go back to the same spot where the incident happened and make an offering at midnight—alone. He had to be alone when he made the offering. He hoped that me and Gopal could accompany him there, to ensure he was safe in case anything should happen to him. He admitted that the place was eerie, and he was scared.

Lim decided to go there that night, without any further delay. He managed to buy all the required things. I called Gopal to accompany us to Sembahwang Park. It took some nerves to convince him to come along. Finally, for the sake of Lim he agreed to come.

That night at ten we were at Lim's house. His wife look worried, but she was relieves as we were going to accompany Lim to perform the ritual. Lim checked all the items to ensure nothing essential was left out. To be certain he gave a call to Mr Juung. Mr Juung read out to him all the required items. Lim had missed out one item; the celery leaves.

We quickly leave to go to a nearby supermarket which would close at eleven. It had old out. We went to another neighborhood supermarket; it had also sold out. We had no choice but to drive all the way to Holland Village, where they have a twenty-four hour supermarket. The twenty-minute drive was worth it. He found what he wanted. We then rushed to Sembawang Park.

We reached there at eleven forty. Lim had twenty more minutes to prepare for his offering. We accompanied Lim to the place where the incident happened. We had three super power torch light with us this time.

Lim quietly prepared all his things on the ground under the big tree. He warned us not to utter a single word when we were there. I saw him lay down one paper plate, and place some chinese cup cakes, sweets and nuts on it. It was bulking up like a mountain. Then he placed three new bowls in front of it. Then he took two big candle and stuck it into the ground left and right of his offerings.

And finally, he took out bottle of Chinese wine and placed it beside the plate. At this juncture, he signalled that it was time for us to leave. I hand signaled to him, if he had got a lighter. He stood up to check his pocket. He put up his palm, shaking it a few times. Gopal quickly took out his lighter, tested it and gave it to Lim. I and Gopal wave at Lim as we turned around and left the place. Lim waved back.

We waited for him in the car. He had given the instruction that after fifteen minutes if he didn't come out, we should go in to find him. Anyway, Lim looked very confident and had no fear at all. The desire to atone for his mistake, and to get cured over powered all the fear.

At a few minutes before midnight, Lim was ready to perform the ritual. He had lit up the candles with much difficulty as his hand was shaking with nerves. He poured the wine into the three new bowls. Then he realized that he had forgotten to bring the salary leave which he had left in the car. He was panicky. At that very moment we dashed in and passed him the leaves and left without looking back. We were just in time.

Lim continued with the preparation. He had to shaft in a few layers of the leaves into his nostril and bag for forgiveness. He had o ask the spirit to pardon him and return his health. He had to repeat this prayer three times. It was not easy—the smell of the salary leaves almost make him sneeze a few times. He managed to control it. He was gasping for breath through his mouth. We were counting down the last three minutes when we saw Lim came out of the darkness sneezing all the way. We're relieved. He was sweating profusely, nevertheless. He was very happy. Lim was not supposed to go home that night. He could either hang around the park or go somewhere else.

Without hesitation, all of us chose the later. Who was going to sit around at that place after such an experience? We proceeded to a twenty-four hour Indian restaurant—'Pratacana' in the Jalan Kayu Area. Lim called his wife to inform her not to worry as he had already performed the prayer and was now on the way to take his supper.

In the car, I jokingly said, 'The Malays believe in ghosts, and we refrain from it. You're the only Indians who are afraid of ghosts.'

Gopal smiled, 'Some Chinese pray to the ghosts to get cured.' We all laughed, 'but the Ang Moh (Causcasian) Ahh! They always pretended to be like ghosts. There are not afraid of ghosts at all.' Gopal was referring to the Halloween Festival which was widely celebrated in many Western countries.

Gopal and I had taken leave from work. No problem, We could sit and chat until day break. For the time being, Lim was looking better and better.

'Did you see anything, did hear anything?' Gopal asked excitedly.

'Hello! You are afraid of the ghost, why you want to know more about it.' Lim said he was under the instruction of Mr Juung not to describe his experience there to anyone.

Actually what happened there was very embarassing. At first it was frightening to see the ghost come angrily to sit right in front of the offerings. Its started to laugh irrepressibly when it saw Lim placing the celery leave into his own notrils and asked for forgiveness. It was laughing hysterically as it was lying on the ground with both its legs and hands waving in the air. Occassionaly he would seep the wine and eat the offerings gluttently.

'Thank God that you people came with the leaves at the right time. I was so panicky and didn't know what to do.' Before we went home, we dropped by Mr Juung's place. He was always ready to receive guests. Lim who felt much better now thanked him a million times. Mr Juung said Lim was lucky as the spirit was ready to pardon him; or else Lim would have been in more trouble and might have died.

'Believe me; it wouldn't have ended there, the spirit would have continued to harass the rest of the family also, if Lim had refused to ask for an apology.'

Anyway, he warned us to be more careful during the Chinese Ghost Month which was due was due to fall start of 8 Aug 2013. During this month, especially on the 1st, 15th and 30th of the lunar month. A lot of believers would make the offering even on a busy street. They would draw a circle with white chalk to indicate the area where everybody should be off limits when the candle was still burning.

We went home happy, mission accomplished. A few days later, a few months later Lim was totally healthy as usual. Anyway, we had abandoned our plan to become anglers. It's a good thing that we had yet to spend our money buying all the expensive fishing tackles.

We now choose a brighter place to spend our time and do sports. We picked up bowling. But, after rolling too much money at the bowling alley, we changed to badminton to spend our time together and at the same time to keep our health—its much better. At times we bring our families along.

THE GENIE WAS MY FRIEND

A Genie is an invisible spirit mentioned in The Al-Quran believed by Muslims to inhabit the earth and influence mankind by appearing in the form of humans or animals with the ugliest feature. Their main duty in this world is to mislead humans not to worship ALLAH (God). They will show some of their power by causing some problem in the family like illness, bad luck, or even financial losses. Those who believe in them and are afraid of them would be under their control.

Since they are in the spirit world not everybody can see them unless they want to show up, or unless you went to their hideout place, known as a haunted place. In this case you're intruding into their territory; they may not like it, and they show up to frighten you away. Some people just can't take his and get hysterical.

However, there are some people who are gifted with the well known third eye. They can see ghosts even in broad daylight. These types of peoople though somehow special, are at higher risk of being misled by the genie.

Genies are known to consume food; their favorite food is bone, how do they consume it? God knows better. There are known to be male and female genies, who marry and and give birth. Some of them live in families and some prefer to be alone and stay on their own.

They can cause the mopes amongst the human being, especially womenfolk and children. They would then ask for something in order to leave the person's body. Otherwise they would remain I and cause health and in some cases mental problems. How do I know all these details? Well! Once I had a friend, a genie. How do I came to know him? It's a story. Let me tell you my little secret now.

One day when I was about forty years old I discovered that I could see the spirit world. My first experience was in my own house. During dinner, my wife would serve the food on the dining table. I was in the living room. I sat on a cushion facing the dining room. My wife went to call all our children to come out for dinner. After sometime I was attracted by a shadowy movement and clearly saw it sitting at one corner of the table. It was concernterating on looking at all the food on the table with it's tongue sticking out with dripping saliva as if the food was served for it. And then it disappeared as soon as my children came to the table.

Immediately we started to eat. While eating I noticed that the same Genie appeared again. Oh! He was joining us for dinner. I stopped eating and before continuing said my 'Do'a' (prayer) aloud. The rest, my wife and my two teenage daughters also stopped eating to obeserve the short prayer—for just a few seconds. When I opened my eyes the Genie had gone, and we continued eating. If my little girl of eight years old is around she will be the one to lead the prayer. Tonight she was staying over at granny's.

One day when I was alone sitting on my favourite cushion. I made a cup of coffee and placed it on the side table. It was still too hot for the throat, so I left it there. I was engrossed with the newspaper. About half an hour later I started to feel that there we're shadows moving beside me. I glanced at them from the corner of my eye. I saw the same figure from the other day. He was sitting on the floor—I beleived he was floating and enjoying my coffee. How was he enjoying it? His long red tongue was lolling out and into my cup of coffee as if he was licking it. He did it a few more times.

Braving myself, I scolded him.

'Hey! Genie! What are you doing?'

I could see he was caught by suprise and unable to escape.

'So you can see me now!'

'What are you doing?'

'I'm licking your coffee.'

Though I saw him lick the cofee but the water didn't recede at all.

'Why are you licking my coffee?'

'This is my fortune.'

'What do you mean?'

'Nobody is drinking it and it's wide open so why not, it's my luck.'

'But, it's mine!'

'If you covered it, definitely I wouldnt dare to lick it.'

'Ok you can have it all.'

'I'll do that. Don't look at me because after that I'm going to pee into your cup.'

'So that's what you meant to do all along!'

'Yes, unless you said some prayer on the drink.'

'What is your name, Genie?'

'I'm Fulani Abdullah.'

'Are you a Muslim?'

'Yes!'

'Why are you so mean as to pee into a fellow Muslim's drink. It's not right. You know that.'

'Honestly, I didn't. I wouldn't do that again. Not in your drinks. But another genie is sure to do it.'

'Hi! Genie! My name is . . .'

'You don't have to say it, I know your full name, even right up to your great-great-great-great-grand-father's name.'

'Really?'

'I'm more then 1500 years old. I was existed even before our Prophet Mohammad came to this world.'

'Where do you live?'

'I live inside your store room with my wife.'

'There are such thing as marriage in your world?'

'Yes! Why not? We also have desire. But, we follow the teaching of Islam also.

'Assalamu'alaikum (Peace be unto you).' My wife and chidren were back, This is how we greeted the home we we're back, and this also how we greeted our fellow Muslims when we see each other.

'Mu'alaikum salam.' I answered, and the Genie disappeared when I went to open the door.

My relationship with the Genie was coming up to a full year. I`ve learnt a lot of things from him. We had had a lot of healthy conversation. One day I told one of my Ustaz (Islamic Religious Teacher) He advised me to stop the relationship immediately.

According to him, the Genie is very intelligent and would misguide a person without them realizing it. For instance he would boast about its capabilities, so that as humans would definItely be amazed. And the moment we asked some favor from him, our faith had gone down without realizing that it is ALLAH (God) whom we should worship. Only from ALLAH we ask for anything that we wanted. I was convinced.

When I told Fulani Abdullah the Genie that I wished to break our relationship, he felt neither angry nor sad.

'You`re making the right decision.'

'How is that so?'

'The kindest Genie is worse than the worst human being. No matter how good and kind we are, we are still worse when compared to the worst humans on this earth. I`ve an ulterior motive to befriend you. To be honest with you, I have my own agenda. I`m waiting for a chance to mislead you. Don`t blame me, that is my main duty in this world.'

'But . . . but! You`re already a Muslim!'

There are a lot of Muslim people who did a lot of evil things on this earth, true?'

'Have faith in God and be a good one. Follow the teaching of The Al-Quran and the Prophet Mohammed. Don't bedevil human beings, especially those who have faith in God.'

'I will. Insha' Allah, Assalamu'alaikum (Peace be unto you).'

'Mu'alaikum salam.' I replied, and the Genie disappeared.

This was the last conversation I had had with the Genie. He never appeared in his physical form again. He did came into my dream once to inform me that he and his wife had moved out from my store room to an isolated cave deep in the jungle of Indonesia.

THE DEAL

Madame Tinah was a black magic practitioner. During her life time, many people came to her to ask for help. She knew a lot of things, she was an all-rounder, meaning she could be a midwive, a faith healer, a masseuse, charm maker etc. Whatever the problem people brought to her, she had the remedy. She would solve it. She never rejected anybody who came to her for help.

She managed to perform all these tasks diligently with the assistance of a 'Polong' (a female genie) who guided her a lot in helping people to get cured from all kinds of sickness. She had another 'Pontianak' (a female ghost) to help her solve with matters of relationships.

She was born as a Muslim. Her parents were also Muslim. Due to life's pressures she had no choice but to embark in the spiritual world for help. Imagine a young woman who was married with two children suddenly having to follow her husband to live in a make shift house just on the outskirts of the jungle. The nearest next house was a kilmetre away. Her husband collected rattan/cane from the jungle and sold it to a supplier—he worked alone.

Almost everyday she would be left alone at home to look after her two lovely children age five and seven. She also had to manage a small vegetable garden behind the house. At times, she would wander a little deeper into the jungle to collect edible fruits and leaves.

As she got used to this kind of life, she had no fear except for the wild animals such as the tigers. Though so far, there was no sign that a tiger had been prowling near her area. She became bold and went even deeper into the jungle. Sometimes, she brought both children, but often she just left them behind to stay in the house if she wanted to go out for a while only.

One morning she was attending to her farm alone at the back of her stilt house. She saw a strange lady walking passed by her farm. The lady was very old with long white hair. She wore charred dress. Her body was bent, and she was using a walking stick. She never thought of anything spooky, she approached the lady to get to know her.

'Hello!'

'Errr!' The lady continued walking.

'Hi! Who are you?'

'Err!' She didn't bother to answer, and continued walking.

Madame Tina felt embarrassed and continued with her work. Deep in her heart she wished to get to know that strange lady as she had no friends at all. She wanted to get a good look at the lady, but she was gone.

That night when she told her husband about it, the husband said 'What human being would there be around this area? Maybe it's a ghost. Don't bother her, as long as she doesn't disturb us, it is OK by me.'

Madame Tinah missed having a friend to chat during her free time. She went to the farm the next morning hoping to see the lady. After waiting for sometime she gave up and was about to go when she saw her from the back stood still a distance away.

'Now, you know who I am'

'Yes! No! No! I mean, I'm not sure,' She answered happily.

'Your husband is right. Aren't you afraid of me?'

'Why should I be. You look like a very . . . very nice lady'

'Good! Good!'

'I would like to be your friend.'

'Sure! I`ll protect you and your family. I`ll help you to look after your farm; protect it from strangers and wild animals. I`ll teach you how to cure all kinds of illnesses, and perform any other works that you want me to do.'

'That`s great.'

'But, there is a big price to be paid.'

There was a few seconds of silence, Madame Tinah was thinking hard 'Yes! Or No! Yes! Or N!?' was playing about in her head.

'Don`t you want to know what it is?'

'Yes, tell me.' Now she had a chance to listen to the conditions first before she made any decision.

'In return I just want your descendents.'

'I have two children only.'

'I know, I want the one in your womb.'

She then realized that she had missed her period this month. Could she be pregnant? She had missed a period missed a few times before, but she hadn`t been pregnant. There was a gap of five years now. She was certain that she was not going to get pregnant again.

'Let me warn you of something! The moment I reveal my name, you cannot break the agreement.'

Without much hesitation she agreed.

'Good! My name is Si Puteh don't reveal my name to anybody. This is our secret. I'll come and visit you everyday. Call me only if you have something important, by repeating my name seven times in one breath, and I'll appear in front of you immediately.'

'OK!'

Si Puteh disappeared in a blink. Madame Tinah sat on the ground disoriented, confused; had she done the right wrong thing? Why had she accepted? Had she been hypnotized to accept the offer? There was no one witnessing the irrevocable agreement between Madame Tinah and Si Puteh the ghost.

That night her husband was very concerned and asked her if she had seen the strange lady again earlier in the morning. She lied to her husband for the first time in her life. She lied again a few more times until her husband was satisfied and didn't ask her about the strange lady any more.

Madame Tinah met her new friend every morning. Sometimes when the two children followed to the vegetable plot, they would giggle when they heard their mother talking alone. The fact was they couldn't see Si Puteh. As days went by Madame Tinah could see the changes in her life.

Her farm was not being the subject of the wild bore or rodents any longer. The farm produce had also increased. The family ate a lot of good vegetables everyday. From Si Puteh she also learnt a lot about herbal plants, and their benefits for curing illnesses. One more thing: she missed her period, started morning sickness, and her tummy was getting bigger. She had forgotten her agreement with Si Puteh.

After two months she knew that she was caught with the baby. She believed she was two months pregnant. She felt that beside the baby, which was growing faster, the tingly, achy breasts was another experience she wouldn't forget when she was pregnant with her two children before. Another symptom that confirmed that she was pregnant was when the morning sickness struck, especially in the morning. The husband knew about it and tried his best not to burden her with household chores. He would come back earlier to look after those chores.

The fourth month when she looked at a little mirror on the wall all she could see in the mirror was a tummy that looked depressingly bulky. Two weeks later she felt the baby starting to move around at anytime now, which she found great to take her mind off her bothersome back. She loved it and smiled whenever the baby moved. Boy or girl? She wouldn't be able to tell as she wouldn't go to any clinic or hospital for a routine checkup. She was deprived of all the modern rfacilities such as the routine ultrasound check.

Madame Tinah noticed something completely different when she glanced at her own belly: the linea nigra, the belly button was really popping out!

One day, when she was six months pregnant, her husband never returned home in the evening as usual. During the whole evening, especially when the sun set, she felt more and more worried about his safety. Near midnight, when both her children were asleep, she summoned Si Puteh. Si Puteh appeared immediately and advised her not to worry. She said her huband was safe and would be back tomorrow at noon.

Sure enough her husband stepped into the house exhausted exactly at noon. Her husband had had a frightening night having been lost in the jungle for the first time. He learnt a lesson and never wanted to work in the jungle ever again. The next day, he told his wife that he was going back to town to look for a job—Madame Tinah happily agreed.

He met some old friends and told them that he was looking for a job. He got only one recommendation which was to work as a Forest Ranger at Gunong Ledang. It may be this was his fate to work in the forest again. It's a devine decree that he couldn't escape.

Considering that he would be provided with accommodation, a barrack—Rangers quarters, he decided to accept the offer. Furthermore, for the sake of his children's educations who were getting on for school agee now, it was confirmed—he would take the job.

His friend brought him to the Ranger's office, and after some interview and jungle knowledge testing, he was accepted. He was asked to come back to sign all the necessary documents in two weeks' times. He left the office a happy man.

His wife was very pleased with the news; she was six months preganant. There was nothing much to be shifted to the new quarters. She had a few pots and pants, kettles and cups, some clothing and that was about all. They did not have any other things that we're worth bringing to the quarters. They didn't need a lorry to move house. A chartered taxi would do. But to get a taxi the family had to walk across the jungle track to reach the main road.

She told Si Puteh the next morning. Si Puteh assured her that she would be always be near her wherever she went.

One morning they started off with some bundles of clothinng, pots and pans. The husband was carrying two bundles. The two children helped to carry a smaller bundle each. He didn't allow his wife to carry anything. They move on and straight along the jungle track.

The moment they entered into the jungle, Madame Tinah felt uncomfortable; she felt as if something was watching and following her from behind. Sometimes it would be on the left sometimes on the right. She felt confident that this was Si Puteh.

After barely half an hour of walking with her swollen feet and ankles, Madame Tinah was so breathless. She need a rest, so all of them sat under a tree. When she felt OK they continued their journey in the quiet jungle. Only the sound of birds chirping, monkeys screaming and the crickets could be heard.

Every ten minutes she took a rest. They were about five more minutes along the main road when the jungle, which was already dark, turned even darker; the clouds carrying rain passed above them. A heavy down pour was expected at this time of the day.

They were already taking cover inside the trunk of a giant tree. Half an hour of rain gave Madame Tinah plenty of time to rest. But that didn't stop the the throbbing pain that she was having. The worse was happening or it may be a false labor symptom, but then there was a lot of blood, the waters burst, and there were contractions that intensified.

She had no other choice except toc lie down on the ground. The more she moved around, the more pain she would feel. She might have been dreaming when she wished for the pain below to disappear!

When the rain stopped, she asked her husband to leave her and the children behind to go and ask for help. She said she couldn't stand the pain and couldn't make it to the main road though it was just another five minutes' walk.

He ran immediately after consolIng her and the two children. He was lucky when he reached the main road that there was an army troop taking a rest by the road side. He approached the sergeant and told him his problem. The sergeant reported to the captain, who instructed four men and a medic to follow him with caution.

For the time being Madame Tinah tried to call for Si Puteh. But, she was short of breath. She only managed to call out tree time, no matter how hard she tried. Actually, Si Puteh had already appeared in her true form: a black woman with long hair, with eyes was bulging out and a red long younger with plenty of saliva pouring out of its mouth. She was crawling towards her. It jumped onto her tummy a few times, causing her to have more pain and bled profusely; she fainted.

With its long red tounge she cleaned up Madame Tinah, who was still unconcious. The two children were crying and sat near their mother. However they didn't see or hear what was going on right in front of their eyes.

When her husband came with the help, Madame Tinah regained her consciousness groaning in pain. The Medic gave her a quick check and gave her a jab of morphine. They carried her to the main road on a stretcher.

The troop had to leave and continue with their exercise, and had to leave them by the road side. They had already called an ambulance which was on its way. Madame Tinah just couldn't thank them enough. An ambulance came about half an hour later to bring Madame Tinah and her family to the hospital.

Madame Tinah was rushed to an emergency theatre. She gave birth to a still-born baby. There was not much regret, as most importantly she was safe and sound sound. Only Madame Tinah knew and realized what was going on and her deal with Si Puteh. She had no regret.

Three days later Madame Tinah was discharged and was brought to her new quarters, a totally new environment. The two children were the happiest. Already they had some some friends to play with. As a mother she was even happier to see her children happy.

Here was where Madame Tinah started to embarked on her black magic activities. Its started when one day an eight-year-old child was suddenly bleeding from the nose. With a piece of a beettle nut leaf she rolled it and stuffed it into the boy's affected nose, and the bleeding almost stopped instantly. A few weeks later a teenage girl had gone hysterical. She cured her instantly infront of some people.

From then on everybody would look for her if they had any problem. As more and more people who came got cured or successful in their wishes, Madame Tinah became more and more popular. Her husband didn't protest as he knew she had helped a lot with the household expenditure and the children education.

During the past twenty years she was involved in the spiritual world she had three more miscarriages. Finally at the age of fifty, she stopped having sex with her husband. Furthermore, her husband who was ten years older then her was not that healthy.

He had stopped working and moved out of the Rangers Quarters, and moved a few kilometres away down the road to a house purchased by their two children who are now working. Here, she continued with her practice. She became more and more powerful as she fulfilled the deal she had with Si Puteh who was forever hungry for human blood.

She started to victimise all her clients silently. Later, her daughter's maid became her victim whenever they came over to stay every month or two. Her daughter didn't believe it when her maid told about the incident where her mother tried to suck her big toe when she was sleeping. She was very frightened. Until one night when the daughter saw with her own eyes a figure who looked like her mother was sucking the maid's toe when she was fast asleep.

That figure dissappeared when she entered the room. She wouldn't dare confront her mother; instead she moved out to the city to stayed with her husband and the maid as she was preganat with her first child. She was warned not to visit her mother, though she believed that a tiger wouldn't eat its own cubs, but she followed the advice.

She only came after the baby was five months old. On that occasion she caught her mother sucking the baby's delicate toe. She took away the baby to sleep with her. Though there was no trace of blood or marks on the toe, she and the maid stayed vigilant the whole night. Ever since that day, she would come and visit her mother occassionally but she would not stay overnight.

Madame Tinah had no choice but to suck her own husband's toe occasionally to satisfy the blood thirstiness of Si Puteh. Three years later her husband passed away. Now she had to feed Si Puteh with her own blood. Almost every night she had to let Si Puteh sucked her toe while she was sleeping—there's no pin at all. Madame Tinah stayed alone until she was too weak to look after herself. She was also suffering from dementia.

One day, a neighbour called her daughter who came over immediately and sent Madame Tinah to a hospital. For the time being she and her brother looked around for an old folks's home to accommodate her.

They got her a place in an old folk's home. She was placed with eight other elderly inmates in a ward. Weeks after she stayed in the ward a lady roomate ran to the staff room saying that Madame Tinah was sucking the toe of one of the patients opposite her bed. Two night duty staff didn't believe it as Madame Tinah was too weak to get out of her bed.

Nevertheless, they went over to investigate. They found that Madame Tinah was sleeping soundly in her own bed. They went over to the bed where Madame Tinah had been reported sucking the toe of the inmate. They checked the toe of the lady who was bedridden and she was was sleeping soundly. They saw traces of blood and bite marks. Madame Tinah was toothless, it was not possible that she had caused it. The lady who made the report was puzzled and returned to her own bed to sleep.

That night the 'kay poh' (busy-body) lady had a terrible night. Everytime she closed her eyes she felt that Madame Tinah had come to her bed and wanted to suck her toe. When she opened her eyes, she dissappeared. The lady became more frightened when she heard a rough voice scolding her,

'I didn't disturb you. Why are you disturbing me?' The lady was crying and apologized to Madame Tinah, promising not to interfere with her affairs.

Madame Tinah would wake up at night sitting on her bed and shaking her body wildy while making a frightening noise. Most of the patients in the room were very old and got used to it, while some of them slept like logs. It was heaven heaven for Madame Tinah, as she went round from one bed to another to sucking their toe, one after another.

Until a week later another lady reported to the staff that she couldn't sleep as Madame Tinah would sit on her bed and shake her body wildly to the left and right. The night staff went over to investigate and saw what Madame Tinah was doing. When they told her nicely to stop shaking the bed, she lay down and felt asleep immediately.

Once a week at about the same time the same thing would happened. More and more patients were disturbed by the scary noise made by Madame Tinah, and the cranking sound of the iron bed being shook in such a manner.

Her daughter was called up and informed about the incident. One day she brought along a spiritual healer who claimed that actually Madame Tinah had died long ago. Another spirit has taken over and made use of her body to enjoy this world. It's true that Madame Tinah had a strong appetite though she was considdrably bedridden. He suggested Madame Tinah be isolated. She was finally moved to a room alone on her own.

Occasionally, on their night round, the staff would see Madame Tinah sitting on her bed shaking her body wildly while making a strange frightening noise. She stopped it when the staff told her to stop. They also used to catch her wondering into other wards standing aimlessly. They would sent for the wheel chair and send her back to her room.

One night Madame Tinah was found missing, she was not in her room, not in other wards or any part of the building. The security guard at the gate confirmed that he hadn't see any body left the home.

Two staff found her squatting down in front of the kitchen refrigerator munching raw meat. They ran away to alert the others. When all of them went back to the kitchen, Madame Tinah was no longer there. They went to her room and found she was sleeping soundly, so innocently. Now they knew another place to look for her the next time she was found missing.

She lived at the old folks home for a year before she finally rested in peace.

DEAR PAPA G

Let me end my stories with this little experience when I was sixsteen years old. One evening my grandfather asked me to accompany him to go to his friend's house as he had been invited for a small feast. Surely I would like to follow. It was food, food and food.

I didn't know that the place we we're going to was in the cemetery area which was about two kilometers away. The sun was already set when he came to fetch me. We walked all the way and reached the grave yard caretaker's house at the far end of the cemetery forty minutes later.

There were about ten people around for the small feast. After enjoying all the food, most of the visitors left in a group except me and my grandfather. The caretaker who was as old as Papa G was chatting animatedly. I was alone sitting on the veranda outside looking at the dark graveyard.

It was nearly midnight when we left the caretaker's house. I believed that Papa G was testing me to see whether I would be afraid or not.

We were entering a total quietness just a few meters away. We were depending on the battery torch light. I've got to admit, I was scared. This was the first time I has walked in the grave area at night. But I didn't want to show him that I was scared. I was walking slightly behind Papa G when I started to smell the sweet scent. I tried to keep closer to my grandad. Its not possible to walk side by side as he was leading me through a short cut walking in between the graves.

I knew that I must not utter a word or send out the signal that I was scared in this kind of situation. But when the sweet smell suddenly dissppeared and a horrid smell was taking it's place, and when I saw a mummy leap about ten metre in front of us, I almost fell onto Papa G when he suddenly stopped. He stoodd still and lit up his pipe.

Then we proceeded when the smell and the mummy were gone. All the way I saw a white cloth flying across the trees and from time to time time a black figure dashed across our path as if it was following us.

What a relief when we were finally out of the cemetery area! We were now on the asphalt road with street light every thirty meters. I asked Papa G,

'Did you smell the sweet scent earlier?'

'Surely! There was the frangipain trees in the area. Nothing to be afraid off.'

'How about the horrid smell and the mummy jumping in front of ud just now?'

'I didn't noticed that. Did you?'

'Why you stop walking?'

'You know I crave for the tobacco.'

'How about that horrid smell?'

'Sorry! I farted, I couldn't control it.'

I just don't know what to say to this old man. I could see him smiling all the way home.

Papa G put his hand on my shoulder as we walk along. He asked me 'Are you still afraidf?'

'No! Not anymore.'

'You see nothing happened, right? There is such a thing as ghosts and spirits. But they can never harm us.'

'But what I saw already frightened me.'

'It was all your own imagination. When you're scared your imagination runs wild and it projected those images that you've alreay heard and registered in your own mind.'

'Oh! Really?'

'Yes! You see why Dracula, the Chinese ghost or Indians ghost didn't appear? What you saw are the image of those ghosts that you've heard about more often.' He buried some sense into my frightened brain.

We reached my home. Papa G was living about fifty meters away down the road. We shook hand and said bye, bye. After Papa G walked a few steps away, I turned and stumbled upon a 'MUMMY' laid down right in front of me. It was only a log. I couldn't imagine who had placed it there in the middle of the path.

My little screamed didn't attract Papa G at all. He didn't even bother to turn his head to look at me. He continued to walk home as if nothing had happened. Perhaps he's laughing away at me again. Or is he a little deaf?